nickelo
PANDEM

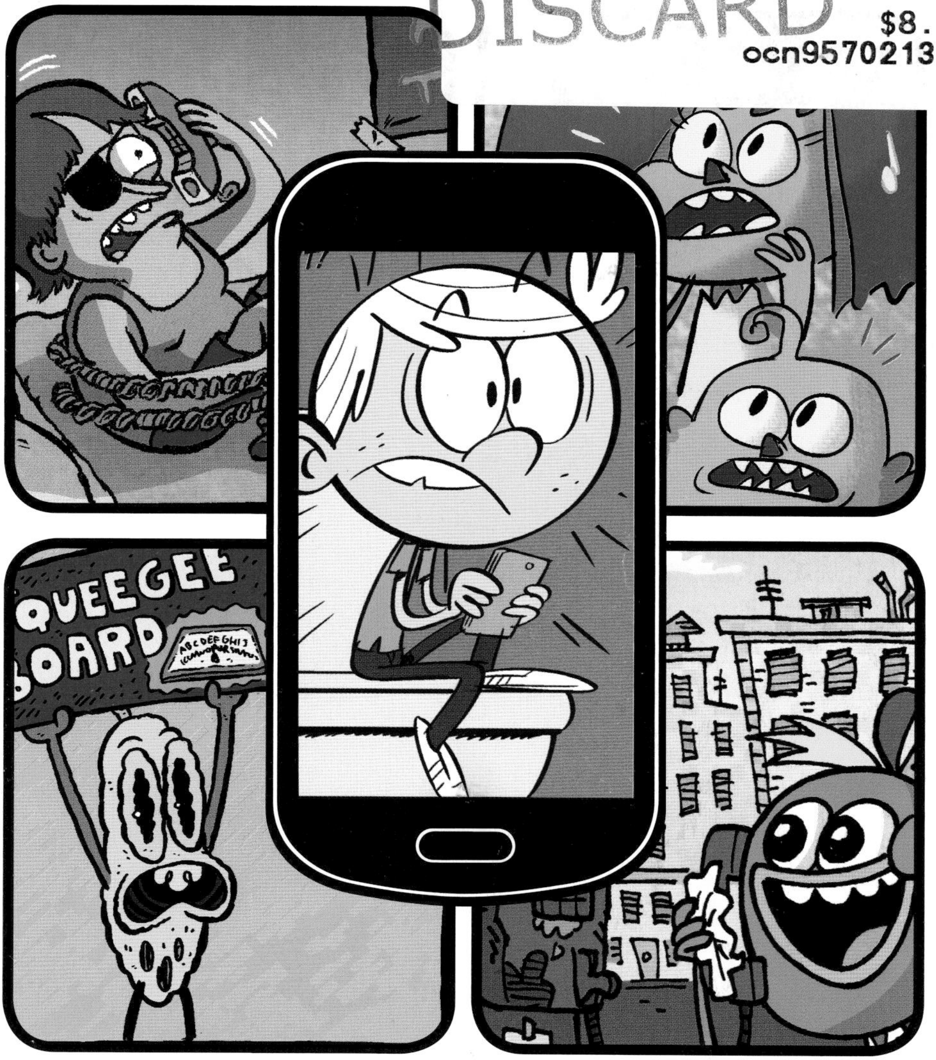
QUEEGEE

PAPERCUTZ™
New York

nickelodeon GRAPHIC NOVELS AVAILABLE FROM PAPERCUTZ

SANJAY AND CRAIG
FIGHT THE FUTURE WITH FLAVOR!
PAPERCUTZ

SANJAY AND CRAIG
#1 "Fight the Future with Flavor"

SANJAY AND CRAIG
NEW KID ON THE BLOCK

SANJAY AND CRAIG
#2 "New Kid on the Block"

STORY TIME WITH
SANJAY AND CRAIG
PAPERCUTZ

SANJAY AND CRAIG
#3 "Story Time with Sanjay and Craig"

BREADWINNERS
JOURNEY TO THE BOTTOM OF THE SEATS
PAPERCUTZ

BREADWINNERS
#1 "Journey to the Bottom of the Seats"

BREADWINNERS
Buhdeuce Rocks the Rocket
PAPERCUTZ

BREADWINNERS
#2 "Buhdeuce Rocks the Rocket"

nickelodeon
PANDEMONIUM!
CHANNELING FUN
PAPERCUTZ

NICKELODEON PANDEMONIUM #1
"Channeling Fun"

nickelodeon
PANDEMONIUM!
SPIES AND DUCKTECTIVES
TOP SECRET

NICKELODEON PANDEMONIUM #2
"Spies and Ducktectives"

HARVEY BEAKS
INSIDE JOKE
PAPERCUTZ

HARVEY BEAKS
#1 "Inside Joke"

THE FEEL-GOOD GRAPHIC NOVEL!
HARVEY BEAKS
IT'S CRAZY TIME!
PAPERCUTZ

HARVEY BEAKS
#2 "It's Crazy Time"

PIG GOAT BANANA CRICKET
Orgle Borgle Selfie Simple-Dee-Doo!
PAPERCUTZ

PIG GOAT BANANA CRICKET
#1 "Orgle Borgle Selfie Simple-Dee Doo!"

NICKELODEON'S HIT NEW ANIMATED SHOW
THE LOUD HOUSE
THERE WILL BE CHAOS
PAPERCUTZ

LOUD HOUSE #1
"There will be Chaos"

Nickelodeon graphic novels are available for $7.99 each in paperback, $12.99 each in hardcover. Available from booksellers everywhere. You can also order online from Papercutz.com, or call 1-800-886-12 Monday through Friday, 9-5 EST. MC, Visa, and AmEx accepted. To order by mail, please add $4.00 fo postage and handling for the first book ordered, $1.00 for each additional book and make check payable NBM Publishing. Send to: Papercutz, 160 Broadway, Suite 700, East Wing, New York, NY 10038.

Nickelodeon Graphic Novels are also available digitally wherever e-books are sold.

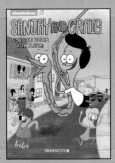

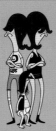

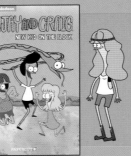

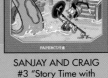

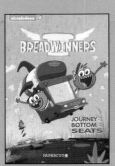

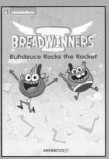

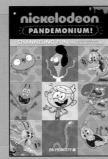

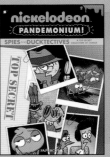

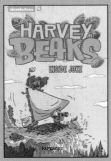

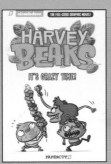

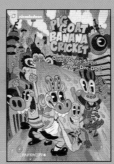

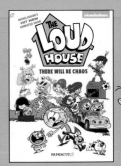

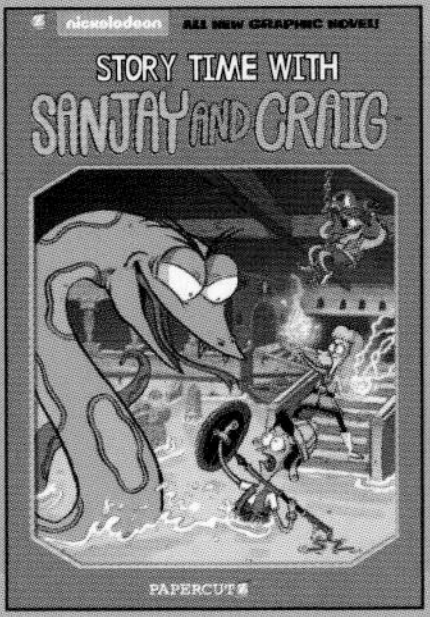

nickelodeon™

PANDEMONIUM!

Lucy's ABCs of the Loud House
5

Community Service
10

Fateway
19

Lower Yeast Side
20

Foo Facts #81- Fire
29

Tumors and Rumors
30

Close Encounters of the Spooky Kind
39

Mollusca Ducks
53

Foo Facts #67 Pirate Booty
55

In Space
56

WATCH OUT FOR PAPERCUTZ™
70

There Will Be Chaos Preview
71

nickelodeon™

⊰ PANDEMONIUM! ⊱

#3 "RECEIVING YOU LOUD AND CLEAR"

"LUCY'S ABCs OF THE LOUD HOUSE"
Karla Sakas Shropshire – Writer
Kiernan Sjursen-Lien – Artist, Letterer
Amanda Rynda – Colorist

"TUMORS AND RUMORS"
Eric Esquivel – Writer
James Kaminski – Artist
Laurie E. Smith – Colorist
Bryan Senka – Letterer

"COMMUNITY SERVICE"
David Scheidt – Writer
Andreas Schuster – Artist, Letterer
Laurie E. Smith – Colorist

"CLOSE ENCOUNTERS OF THE SPOOKY KIND"
Eric Esquivel – Writer
David DeGrand – Artist
Laurie E. Smith, Matt Herms – Colorists
Tom Orzechowski – Letterer

"FATEWAY"
Dale Malinowski – Writer
Sam Spina – Artist, Letterer
Laurie E. Smith – Colorist

"MOLLUSCA DUCKS"
Dale Malinowski – Writer
Gary Fields – Artist
Laurie E. Smith – Colorist
Bryan Senka – Letterer

"LOWER YEAST SIDE"
Eric Esquivel – Writer
Gary Fields – Artist
Laurie E. Smith – Colorist
Bryan Senka – Letterer

"FOO FACTS #67 – PIRATE BOOTY"
Carson Montgomery – Writer
Andreas Schuster – Artist, Colorist, Letterer

"FOO FACTS #81– FIRE"
Carson Montgomery – Writer
Andreas Schuster – Artist, Colorist, Letterer

"PIG GOAT BANANA CRICKET IN SPACE"
Eric Esquivel – Writer
Andreas Schuster – Artist, Letterer
Matt Herms, Laurie E. Smith – Colorists

"SHOCKER"
Miguel Puga – Writer, Artist, Letterer
Amanda Rynda – Colorist

Breadwinners created by Gary "Doodles" DiRaffeale and Steve Borst
Harvey Beaks created by C.H. Greenblatt
Pig Goat Banana Cricket created by Johnny Ryan and Dave Cooper
Sanjay and Craig created by Jim Dirschberger, Jay Howell, and Andreas Trolf
The Loud House created by Chris Savino
Chris Savino and Andreas Schuster – Cover Artists
James Salerno – Sr. Art Director/Nickelodeon
Dawn Guzzo – Design/Production Coordination
Jeff Whitman – Editor
Joan Hilty – Comics Editor/Nickelodeon
Jim Salicrup
Editor-in-Chief

ISBN: 978-1-62991-755-9 paperback edition
ISBN: 978-1-62991-756-6 hardcover edition

Papercutz books may be purchased for business or promotional use. For information on bulk
purchases please contact Macmillan Corporate and Premium Sales Department at (800) 221-7945 x5442.

Printed in China
August 2017

Distributed by Macmillan
First Printing

"LUCY'S ABCs OF THE LOUD HOUSE"

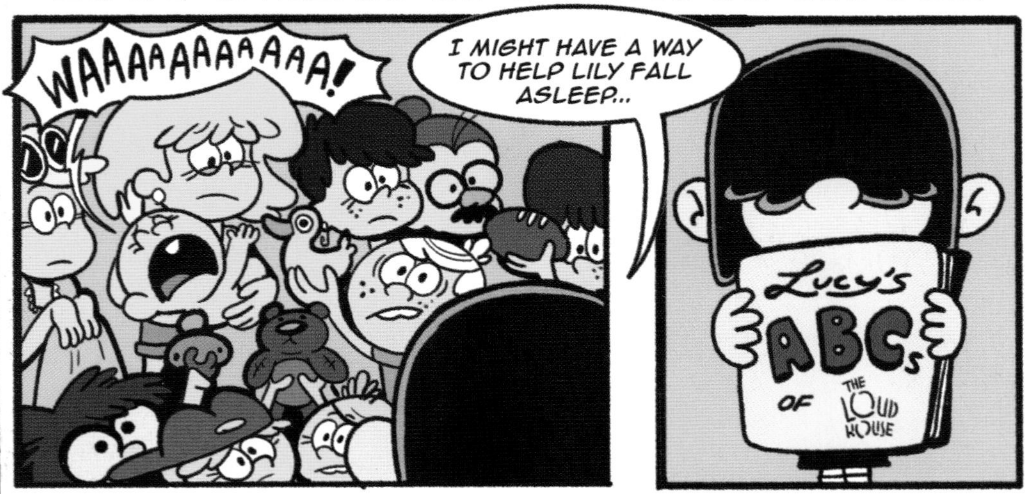
WAAAAAAAAAAA!
I MIGHT HAVE A WAY TO HELP LILY FALL ASLEEP...
Lucy's ABCs OF THE LOUD HOUSE

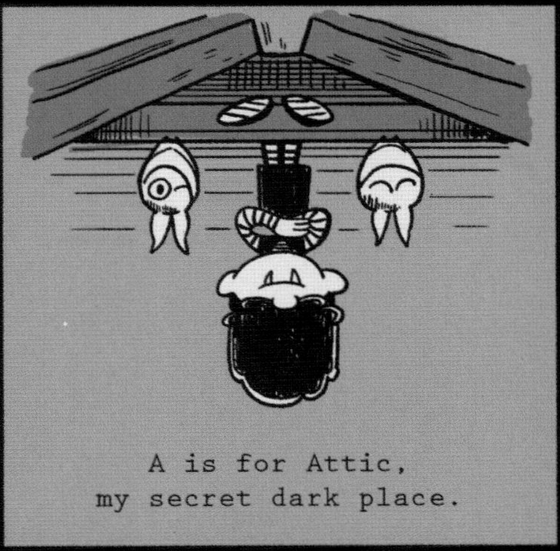
A is for Attic,
my secret dark place.

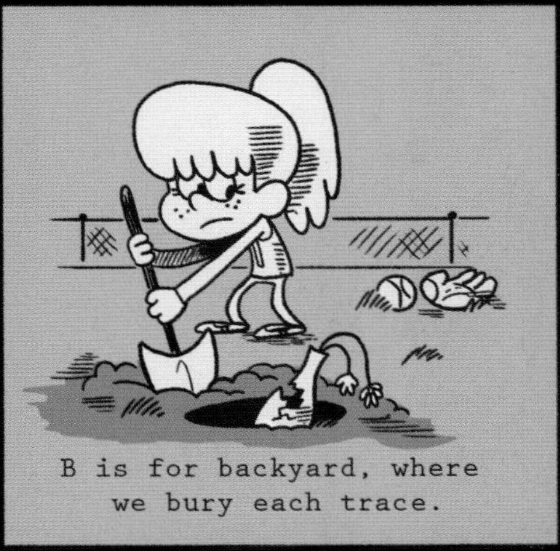
B is for backyard, where
we bury each trace.

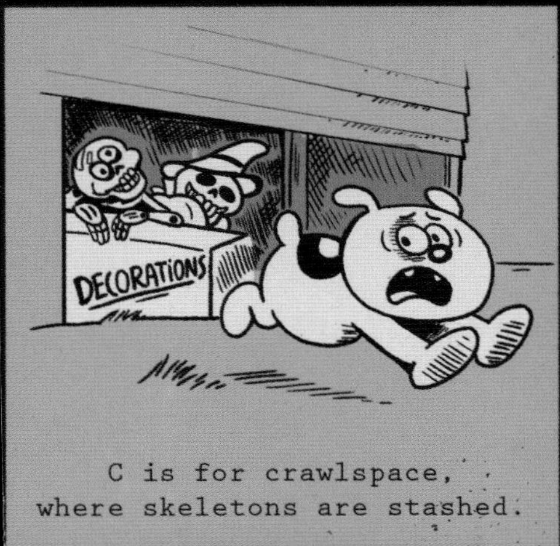
DECORATIONS
C is for crawlspace,
where skeletons are stashed.

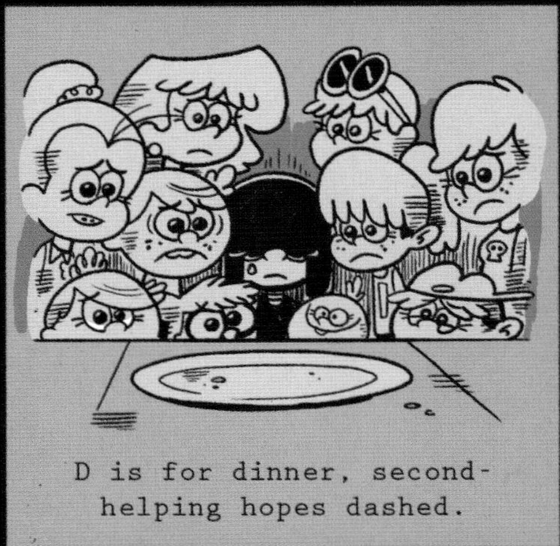
D is for dinner, second-
helping hopes dashed.

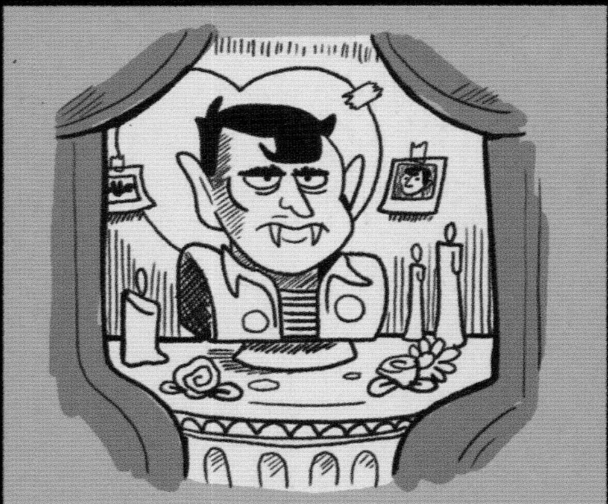

E is for Edwin shrine,
safe in my room.

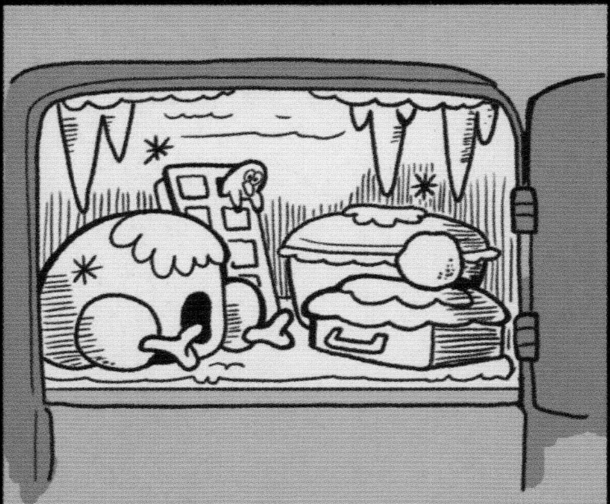

F is for freezer, where
leftovers meet their doom.

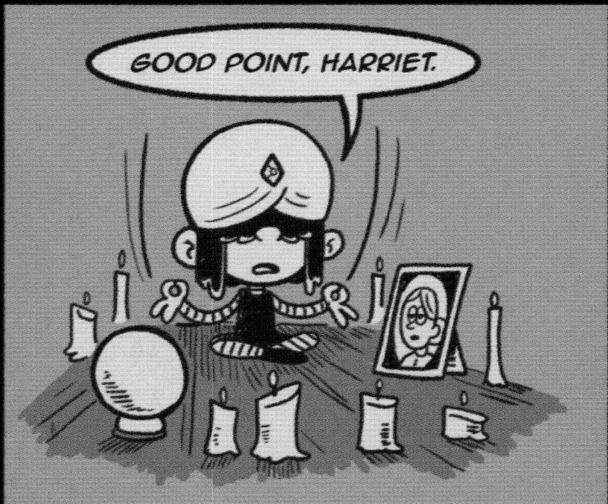
GOOD POINT, HARRIET.

G is for Great Grandma,
of whom I'm so fond.

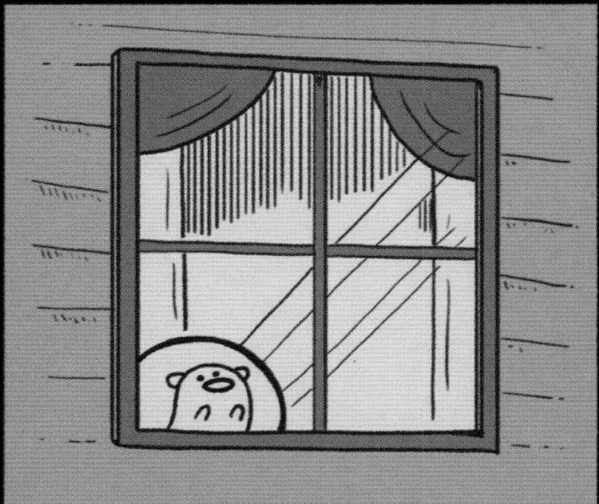

H is for hamster ball,
Geo can't get beyond.

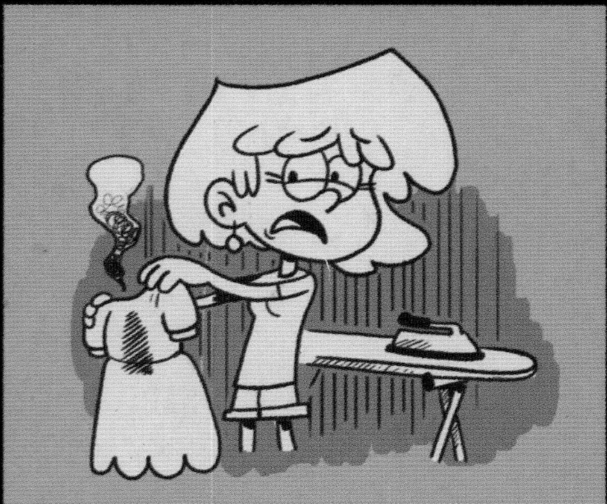

I is for iron,
feared by our clothes.

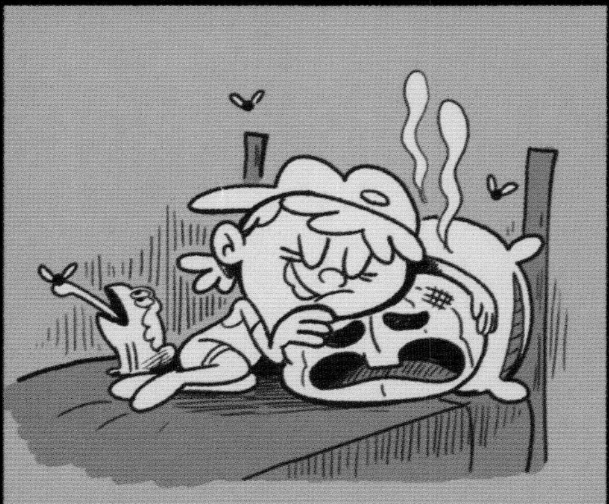

J is for Jack-O-Lantern
that got really gross.

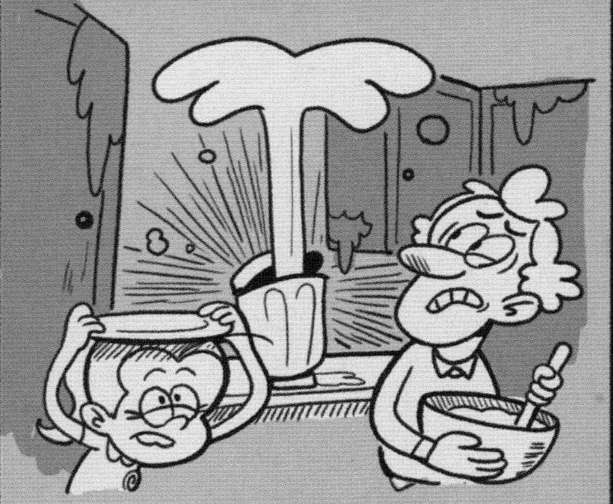

K is for kitchen,
whose hazards are various.

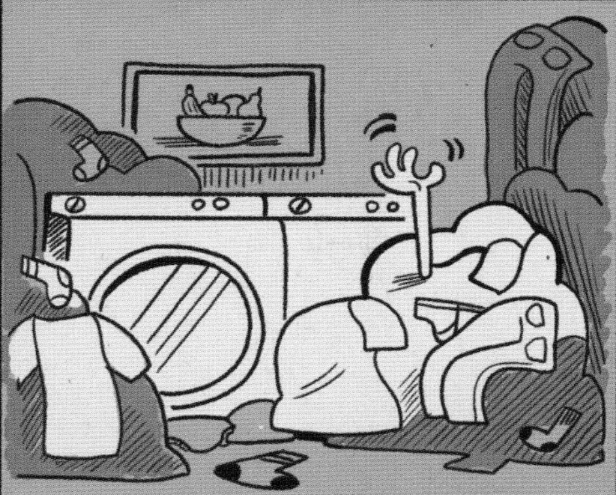

L is for laundry that
threatens to bury us.

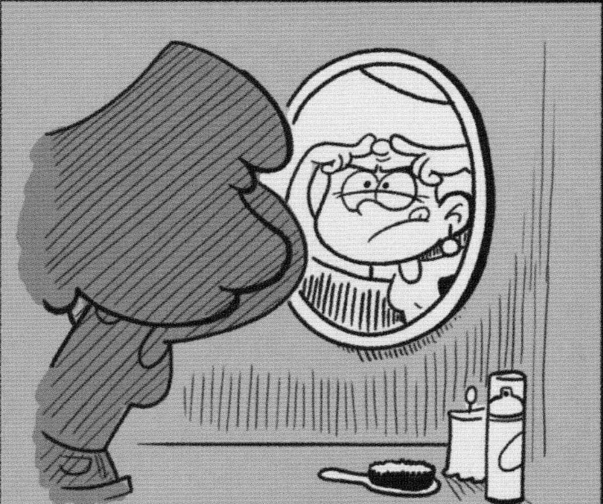

M is for mirror and
the horrors it's seen.

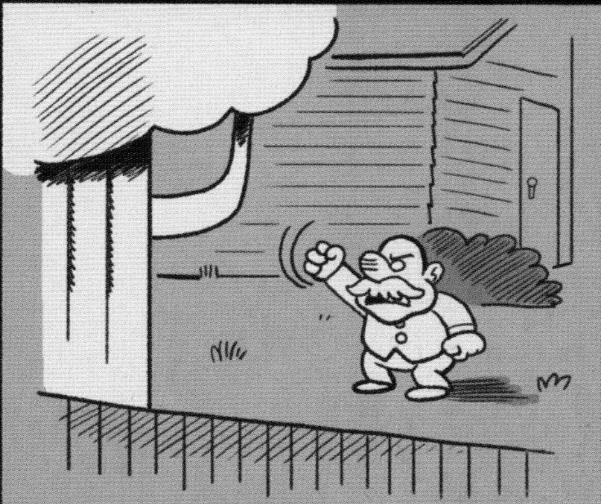

N is for next-door neighbors
who're totally mean.

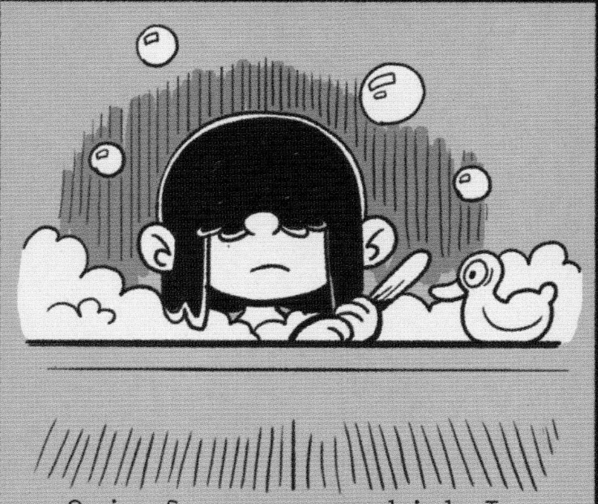

O is for omens, which I
see in my bubble brew.

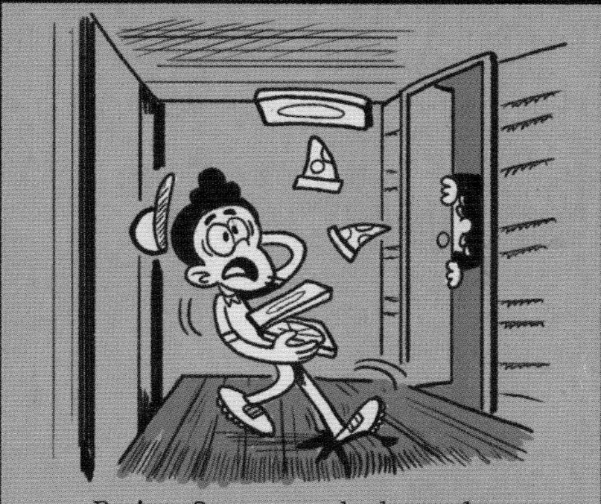

P is for porch boards,
rotted right through.

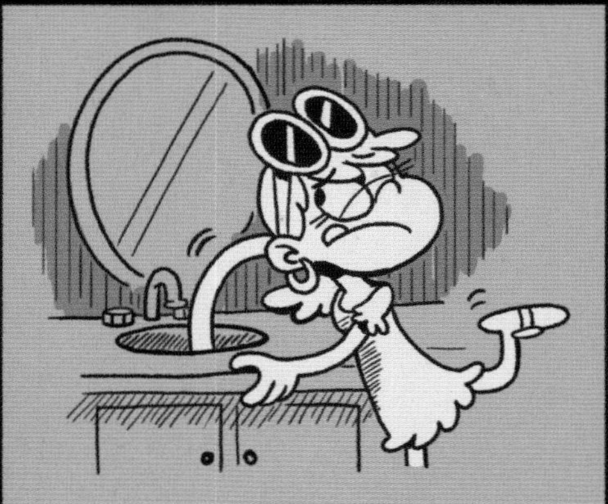

Q is for quarters
lost down the drain.

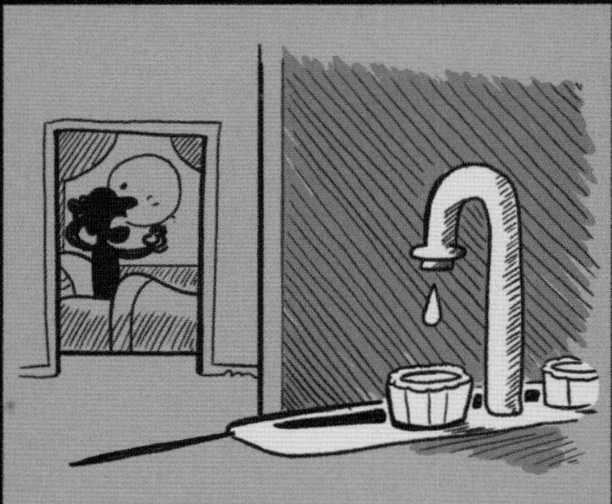

R is for runny faucet-
it drives Dad insane!

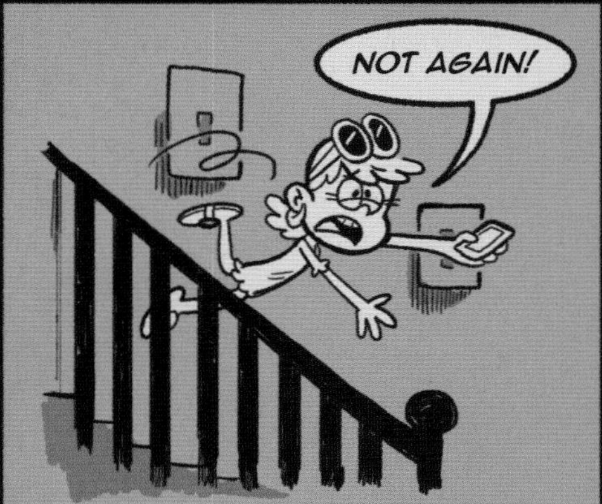
NOT AGAIN!

S is for staircase,
where Leni pratfalls.

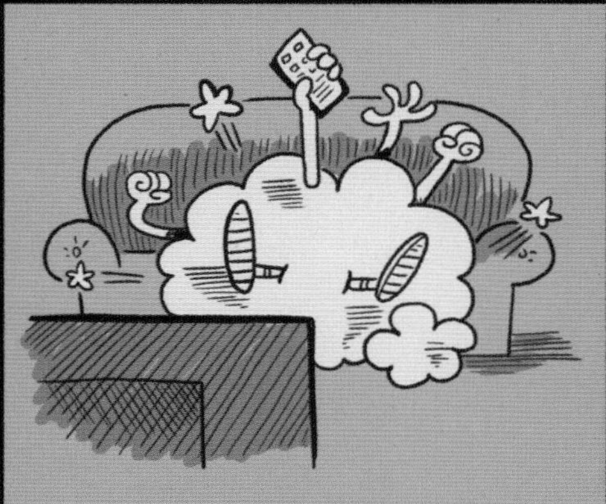

T is for TV remote,
which causes brawls.

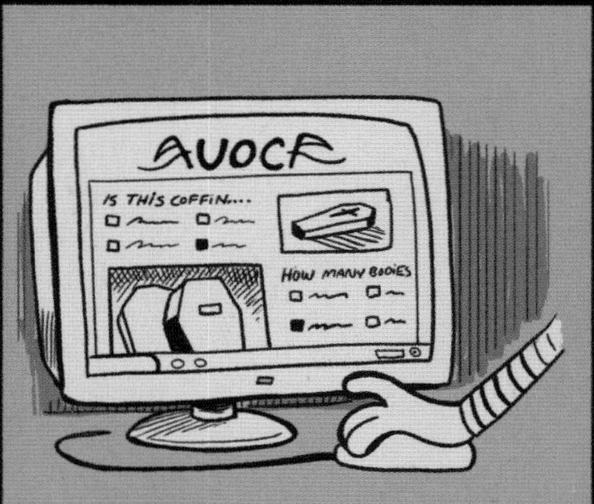
IS THIS COFFIN....
HOW MANY BODIES

U is for undertaker's
online course...

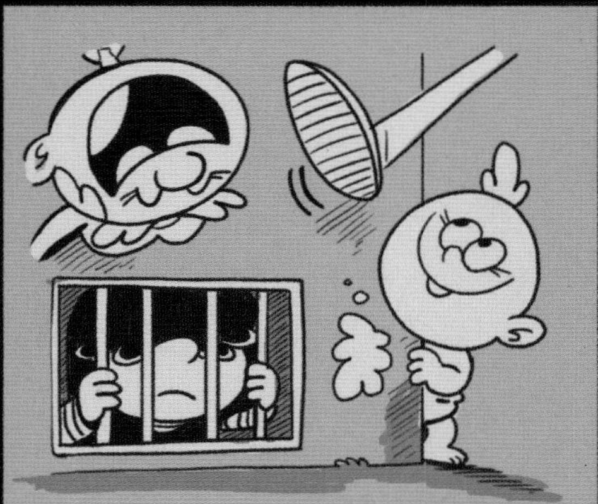

V is for vents, when
chaos is in full force.

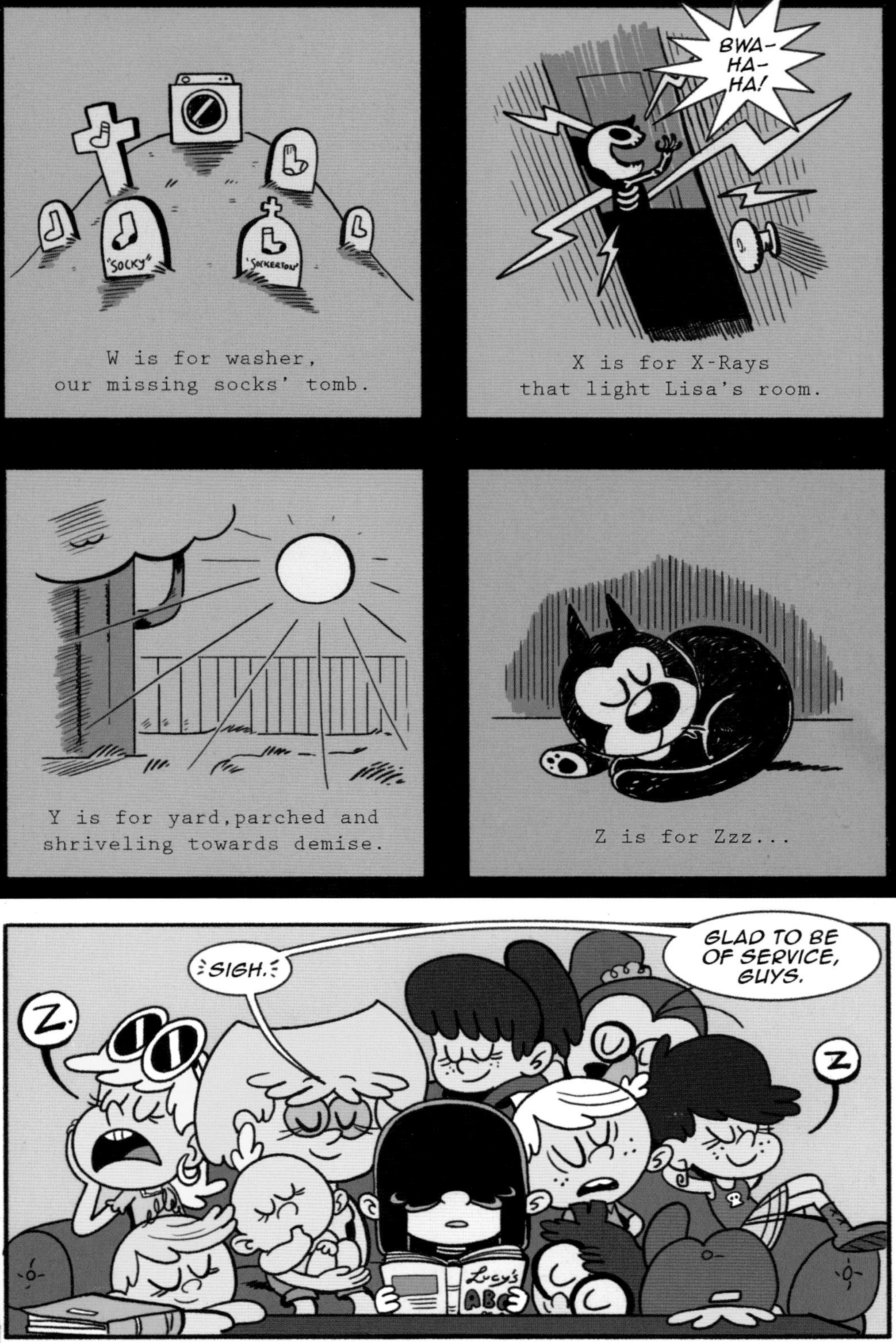
"SOCKY"
'SOCKERTON'
W is for washer,
our missing socks' tomb.
BWA-HA-HA!
X is for X-Rays
that light Lisa's room.
Y is for yard,parched and
shriveling towards demise.
Z is for Zzz...
Z
SIGH.
GLAD TO BE OF SERVICE, GUYS.
Z
Lucy's ABC

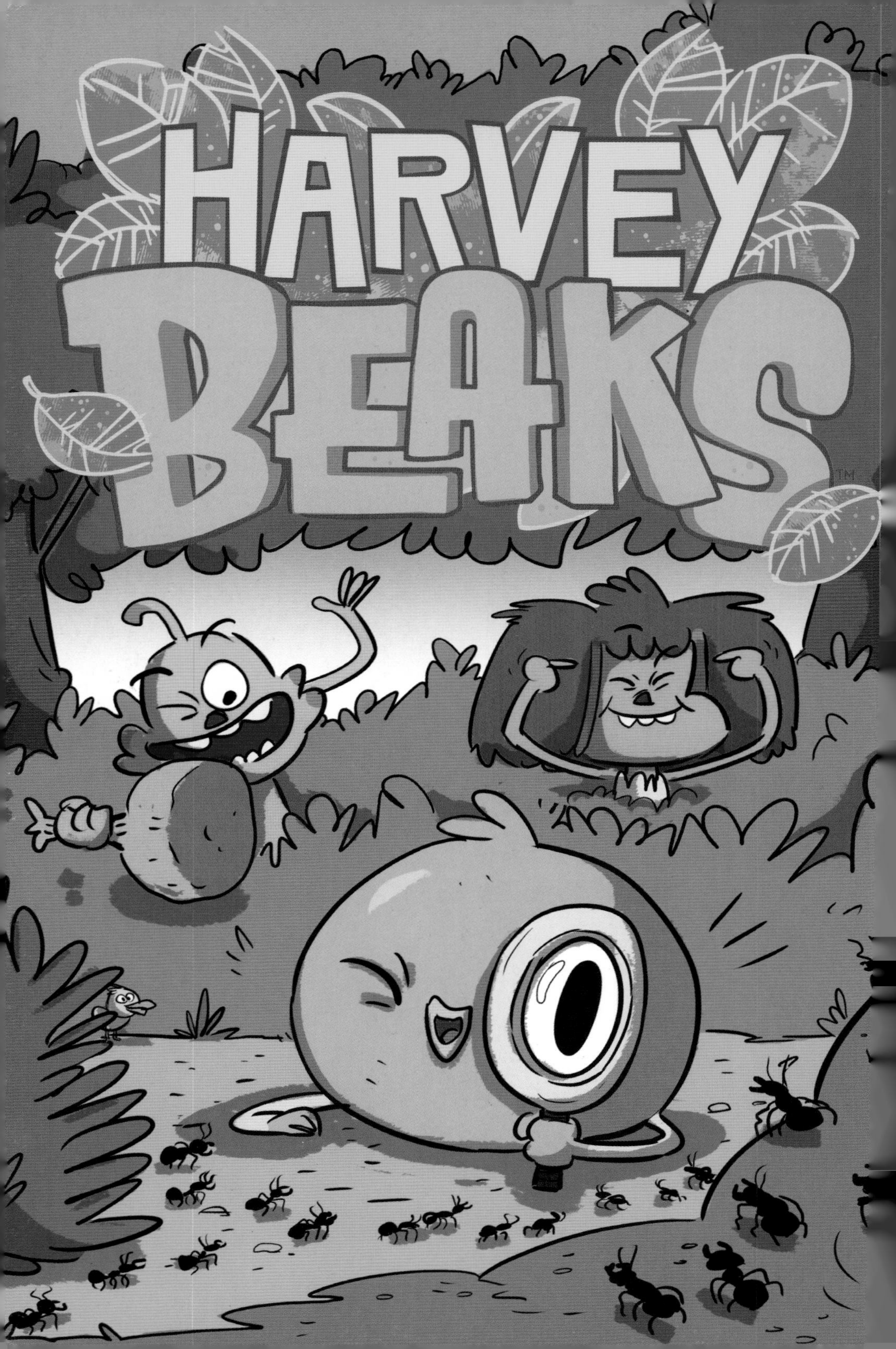
HARVEY
BEAKS™

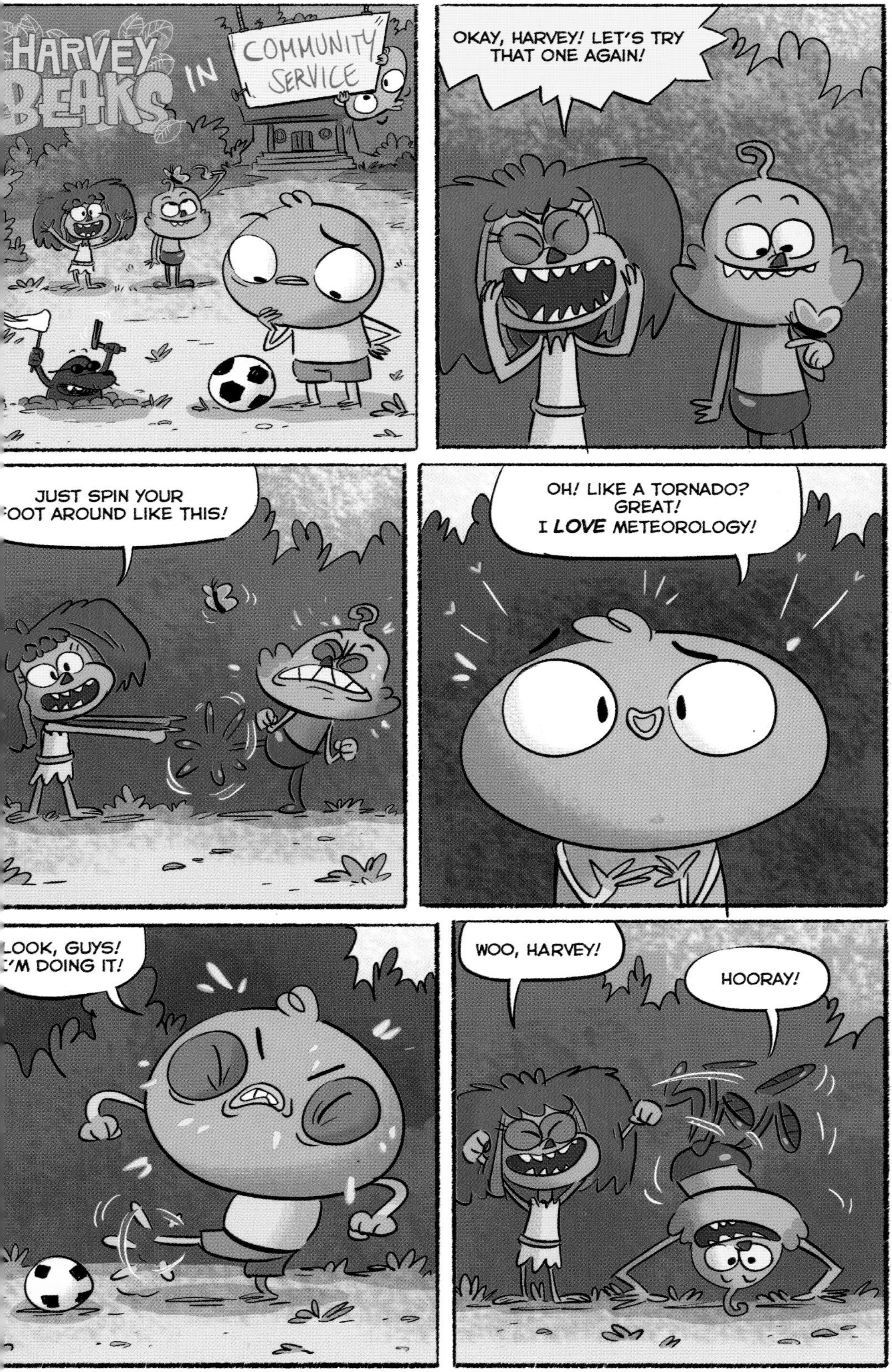
HARVEY BEAKS IN
COMMUNITY SERVICE
OKAY, HARVEY! LET'S TRY THAT ONE AGAIN!
JUST SPIN YOUR FOOT AROUND LIKE THIS!
OH! LIKE A TORNADO? GREAT! I *LOVE* METEOROLOGY!
LOOK, GUYS! I'M DOING IT!
WOO, HARVEY!
HOORAY!

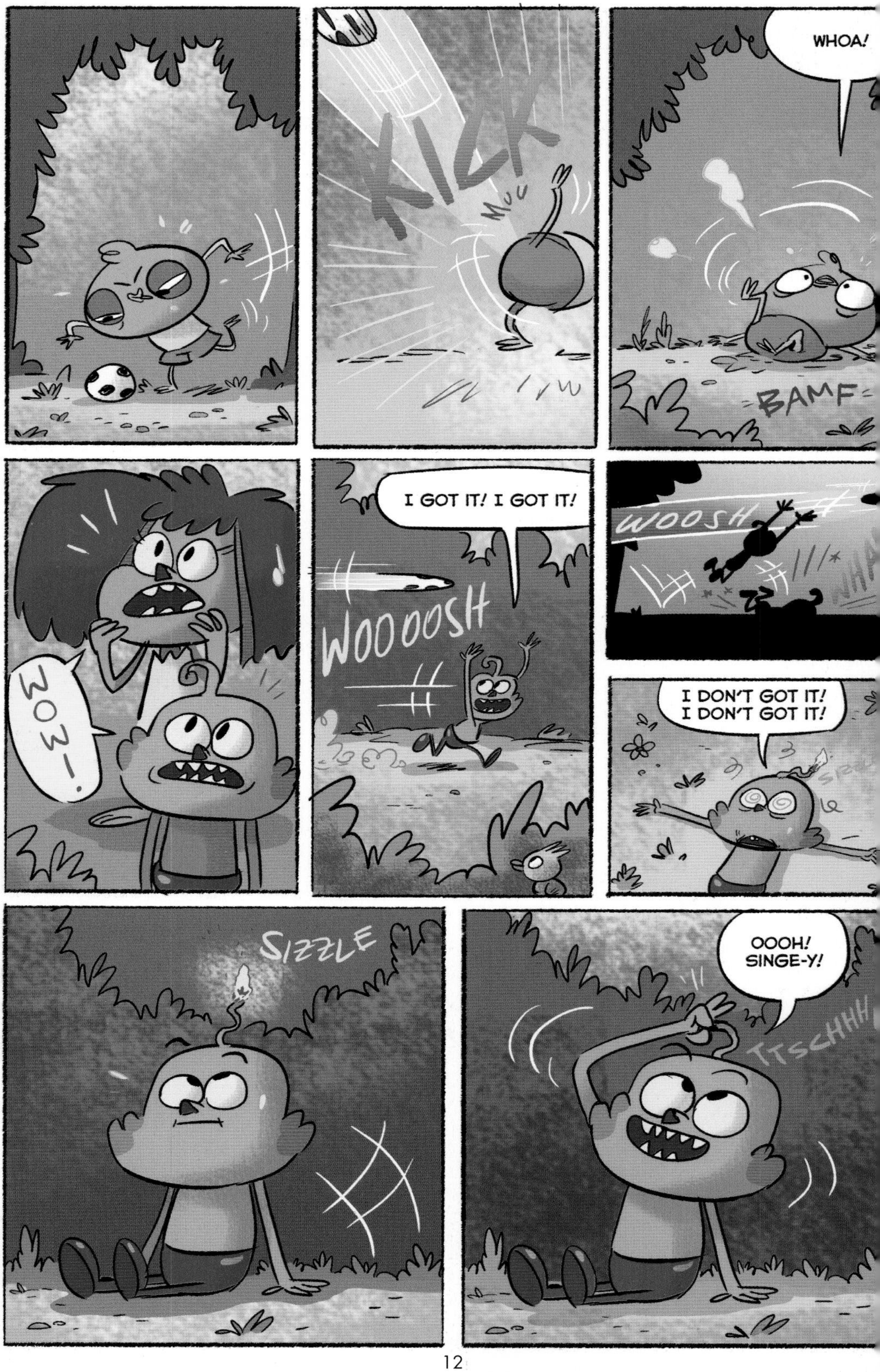
KICK
WHOA!
BAMF
WOW!
I GOT IT! I GOT IT!
WOOOOSH
WOOSH
I DON'T GOT IT!
I DON'T GOT IT!
SIZZLE
OOOH!
SINGE-Y!

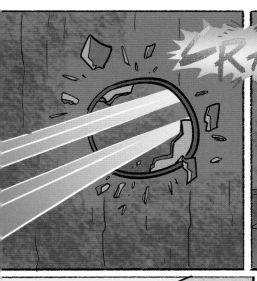

CRASH

GRENADE! RANDL, HIT THE DECK!

MA! GET UP! IT'S JUST A SOCCER BALL!

I COULD HAVE SWORN IT WAS *ENEMY FIRE!*

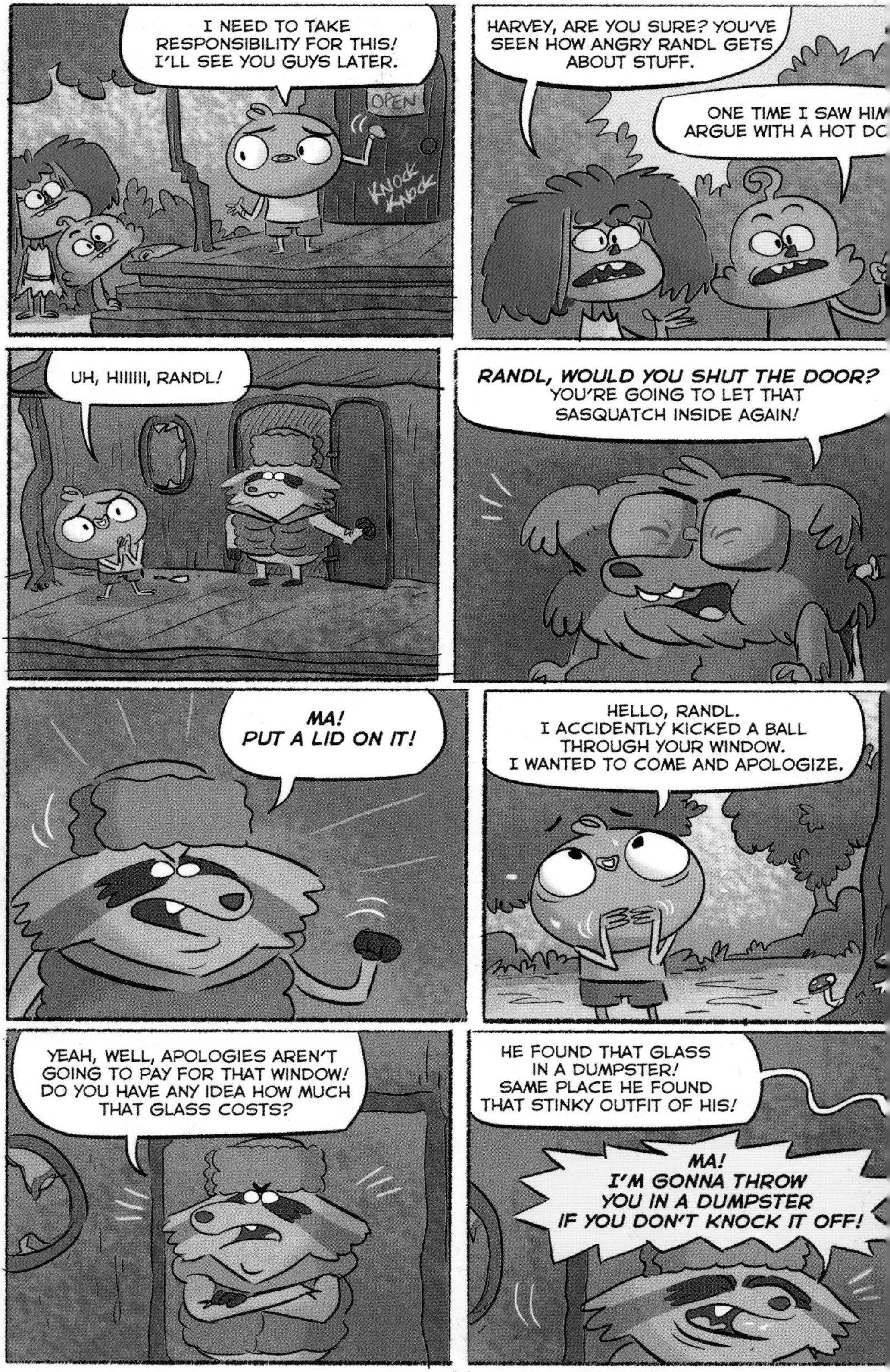
I NEED TO TAKE RESPONSIBILITY FOR THIS! I'LL SEE YOU GUYS LATER.
OPEN
KNOCK KNOCK
HARVEY, ARE YOU SURE? YOU'VE SEEN HOW ANGRY RANDL GETS ABOUT STUFF.
ONE TIME I SAW HIM ARGUE WITH A HOT DO
UH, HIIIIII, RANDL!
RANDL, WOULD YOU SHUT THE DOOR? YOU'RE GOING TO LET THAT SASQUATCH INSIDE AGAIN!
MA! PUT A LID ON IT!
HELLO, RANDL. I ACCIDENTLY KICKED A BALL THROUGH YOUR WINDOW. I WANTED TO COME AND APOLOGIZE.
YEAH, WELL, APOLOGIES AREN'T GOING TO PAY FOR THAT WINDOW! DO YOU HAVE ANY IDEA HOW MUCH THAT GLASS COSTS?
HE FOUND THAT GLASS IN A DUMPSTER! SAME PLACE HE FOUND THAT STINKY OUTFIT OF HIS!
MA! I'M GONNA THROW YOU IN A DUMPSTER IF YOU DON'T KNOCK IT OFF!

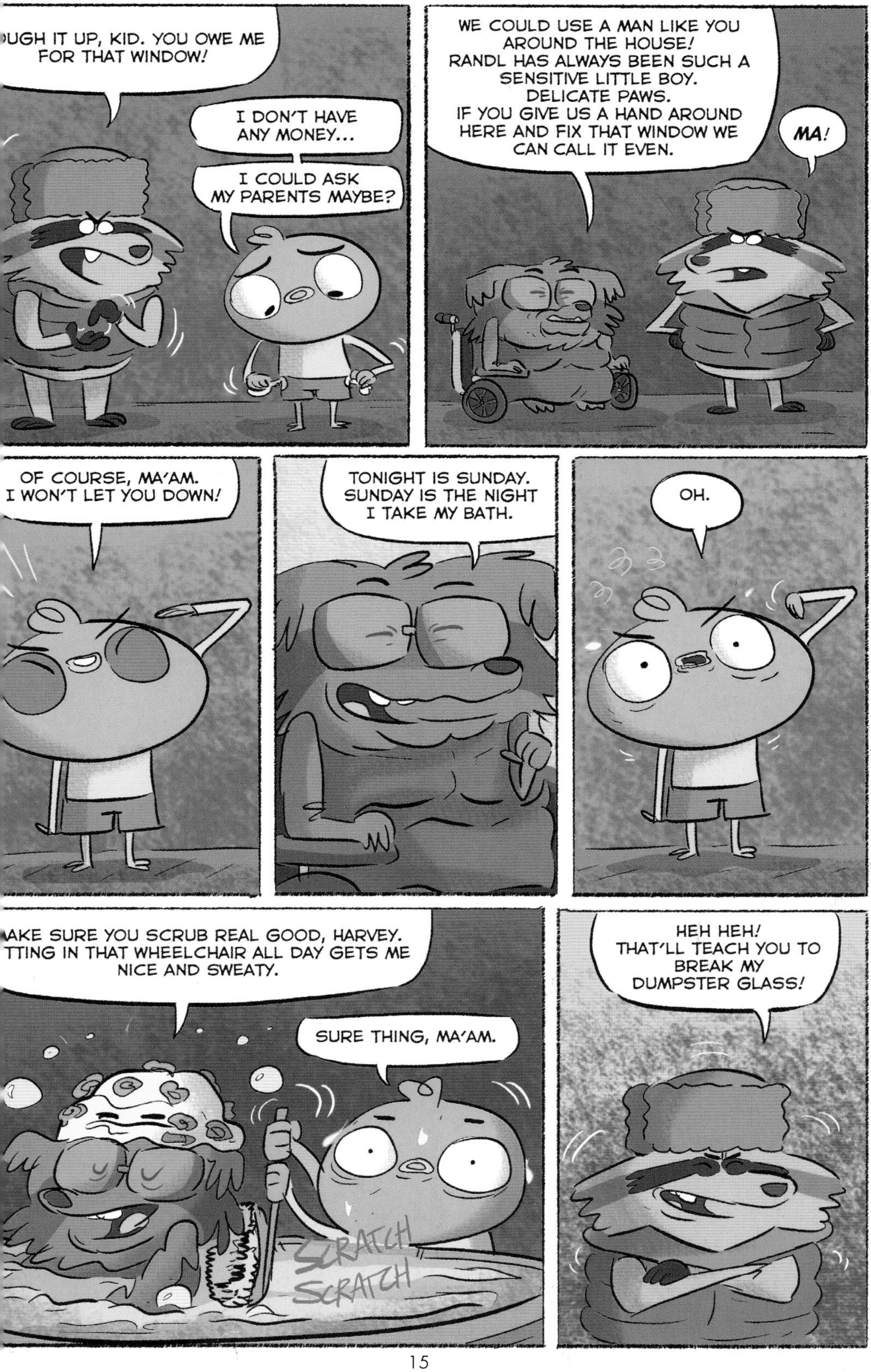
UGH IT UP, KID. YOU OWE ME FOR THAT WINDOW!
I DON'T HAVE ANY MONEY...
I COULD ASK MY PARENTS MAYBE?
WE COULD USE A MAN LIKE YOU AROUND THE HOUSE! RANDL HAS ALWAYS BEEN SUCH A SENSITIVE LITTLE BOY. DELICATE PAWS. IF YOU GIVE US A HAND AROUND HERE AND FIX THAT WINDOW WE CAN CALL IT EVEN.
MA!
OF COURSE, MA'AM. I WON'T LET YOU DOWN!
TONIGHT IS SUNDAY. SUNDAY IS THE NIGHT I TAKE MY BATH.
OH.
AKE SURE YOU SCRUB REAL GOOD, HARVEY. TTING IN THAT WHEELCHAIR ALL DAY GETS ME NICE AND SWEATY.
SURE THING, MA'AM.
SCRATCH SCRATCH
HEH HEH! THAT'LL TEACH YOU TO BREAK MY DUMPSTER GLASS!

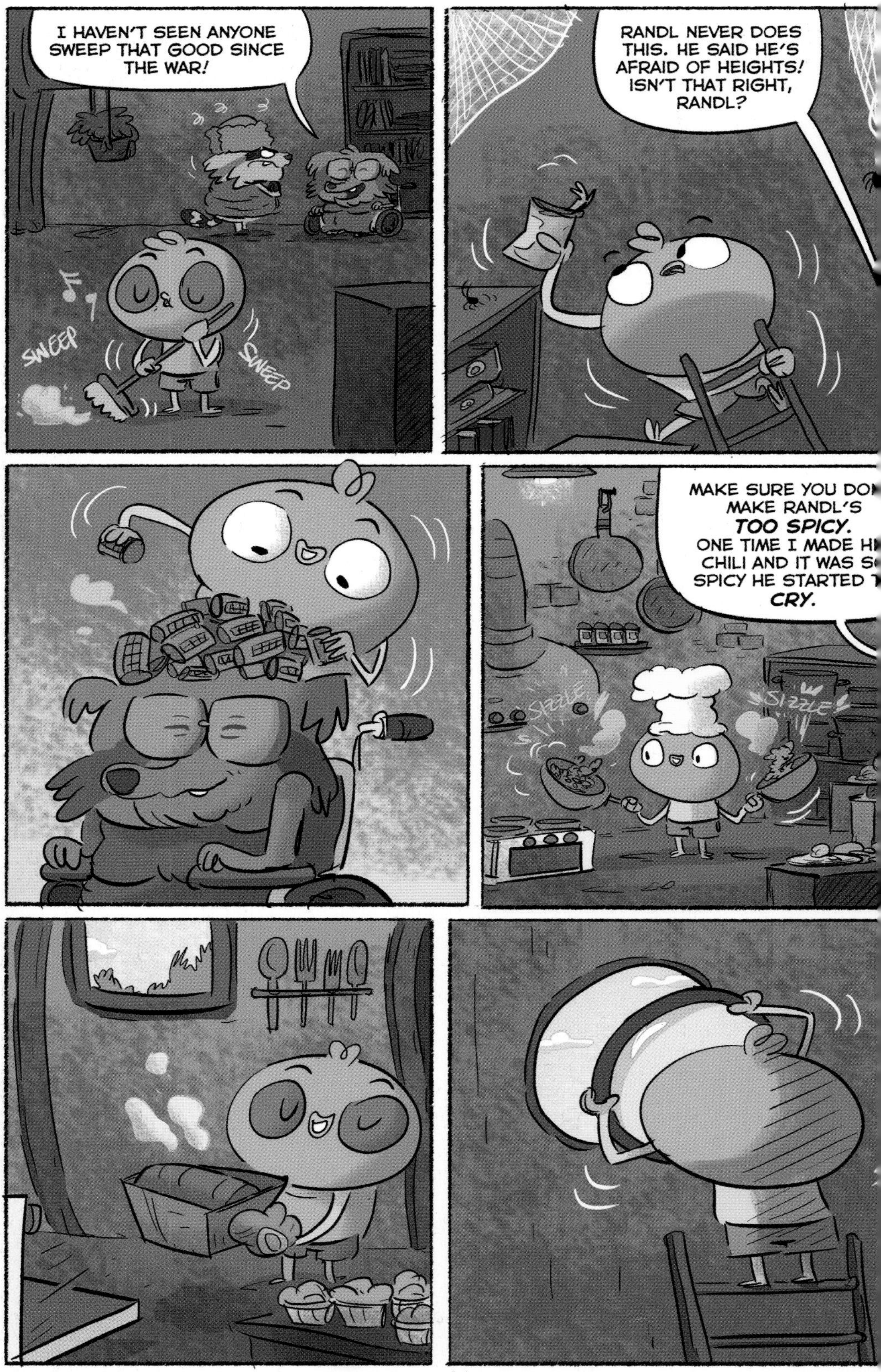

I HAVEN'T SEEN ANYONE SWEEP THAT GOOD SINCE THE WAR!
SWEEP
SWEEP
RANDL NEVER DOES THIS. HE SAID HE'S AFRAID OF HEIGHTS! ISN'T THAT RIGHT, RANDL?
MAKE SURE YOU DO
MAKE RANDL'S
TOO SPICY.
ONE TIME I MADE H
CHILI AND IT WAS S
SPICY HE STARTED
CRY.
SIZZLE
SIZZLE

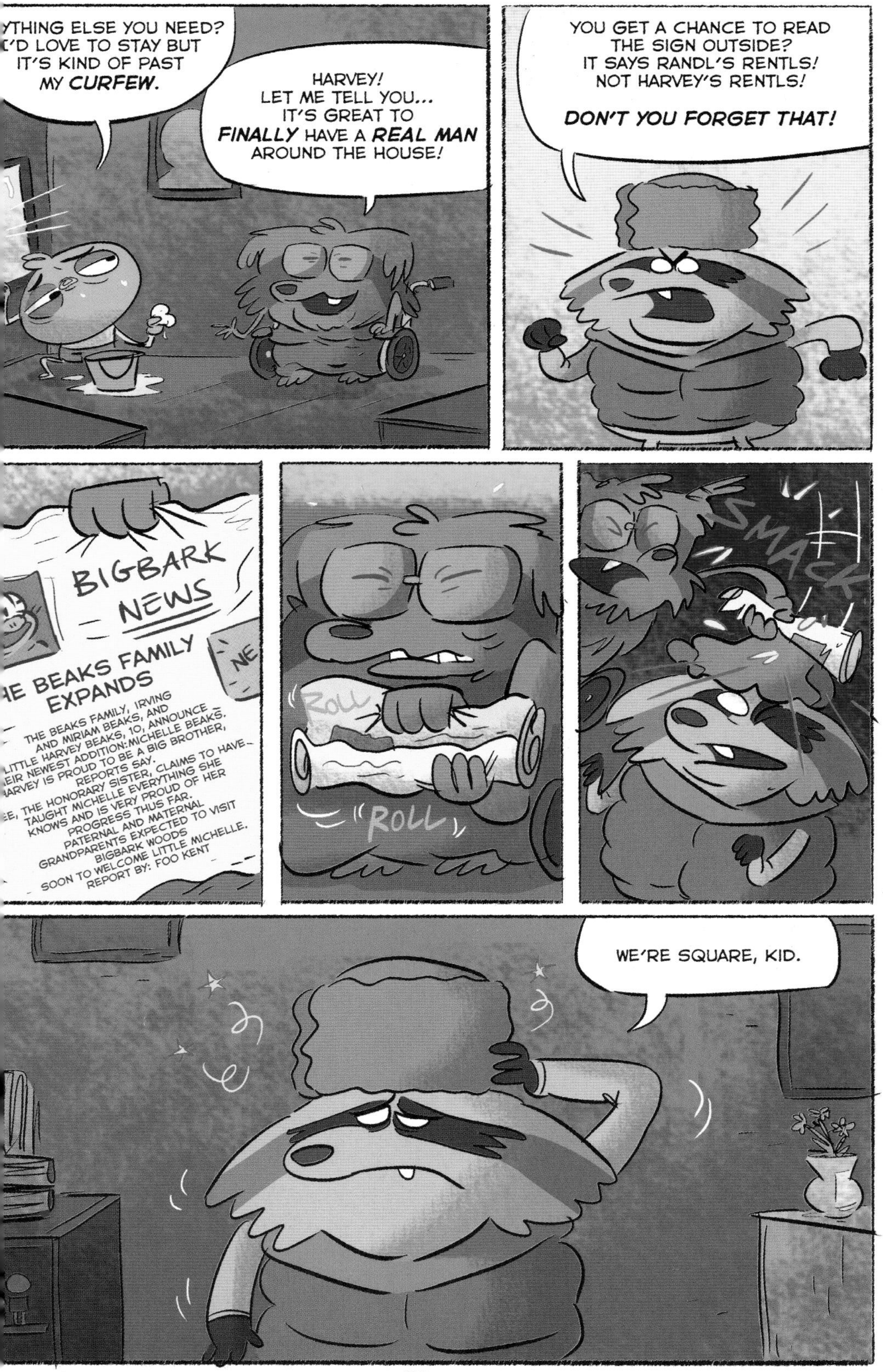
YTHING ELSE YOU NEED? I'D LOVE TO STAY BUT IT'S KIND OF PAST MY **CURFEW.**
HARVEY! LET ME TELL YOU... IT'S GREAT TO **FINALLY** HAVE A **REAL MAN** AROUND THE HOUSE!
YOU GET A CHANCE TO READ THE SIGN OUTSIDE? IT SAYS RANDL'S RENTLS! NOT HARVEY'S RENTLS!
DON'T YOU FORGET THAT!
BIGBARK NEWS
HE BEAKS FAMILY EXPANDS
THE BEAKS FAMILY, IRVING AND MIRIAM BEAKS, AND LITTLE HARVEY BEAKS, 10, ANNOUNCE EIR NEWEST ADDITION: MICHELLE BEAKS. ARVEY IS PROUD TO BE A BIG BROTHER, REPORTS SAY.
EE, THE HONORARY SISTER, CLAIMS TO HAVE TAUGHT MICHELLE EVERYTHING SHE KNOWS AND IS VERY PROUD OF HER PROGRESS THUS FAR.
PATERNAL AND MATERNAL GRANDPARENTS EXPECTED TO VISIT BIGBARK WOODS SOON TO WELCOME LITTLE MICHELLE.
REPORT BY: FOO KENT
NE
ROLL
ROLL
SMACK
WE'RE SQUARE, KID.

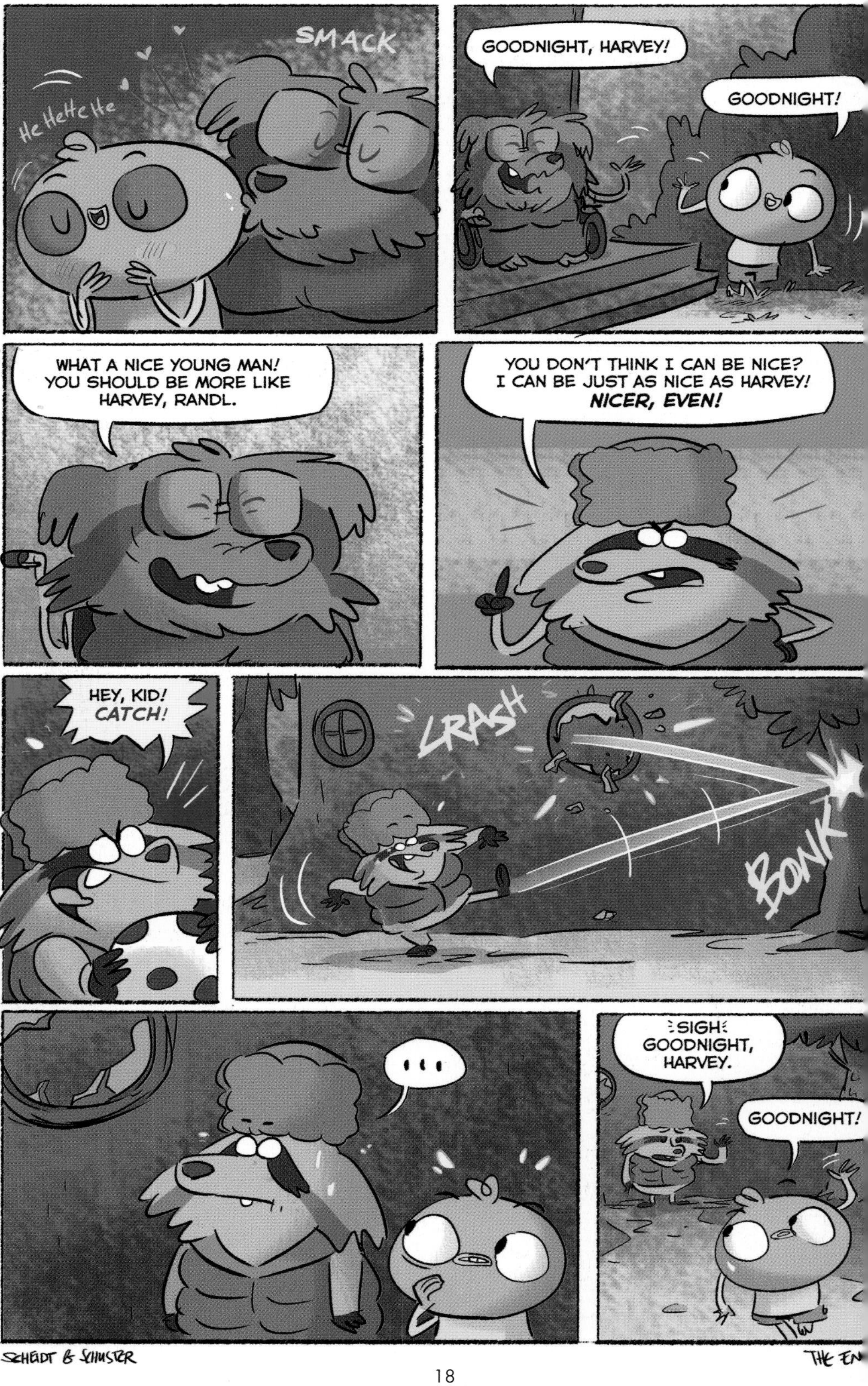
SMACK
He HeHe He
GOODNIGHT, HARVEY!
GOODNIGHT!
WHAT A NICE YOUNG MAN! YOU SHOULD BE MORE LIKE HARVEY, RANDL.
YOU DON'T THINK I CAN BE NICE? I CAN BE JUST AS NICE AS HARVEY! NICER, EVEN!
HEY, KID! CATCH!
CRASH
BONK
...
SIGH GOODNIGHT, HARVEY.
GOODNIGHT!
SCHEIDT & SCHUSTER
THE EN

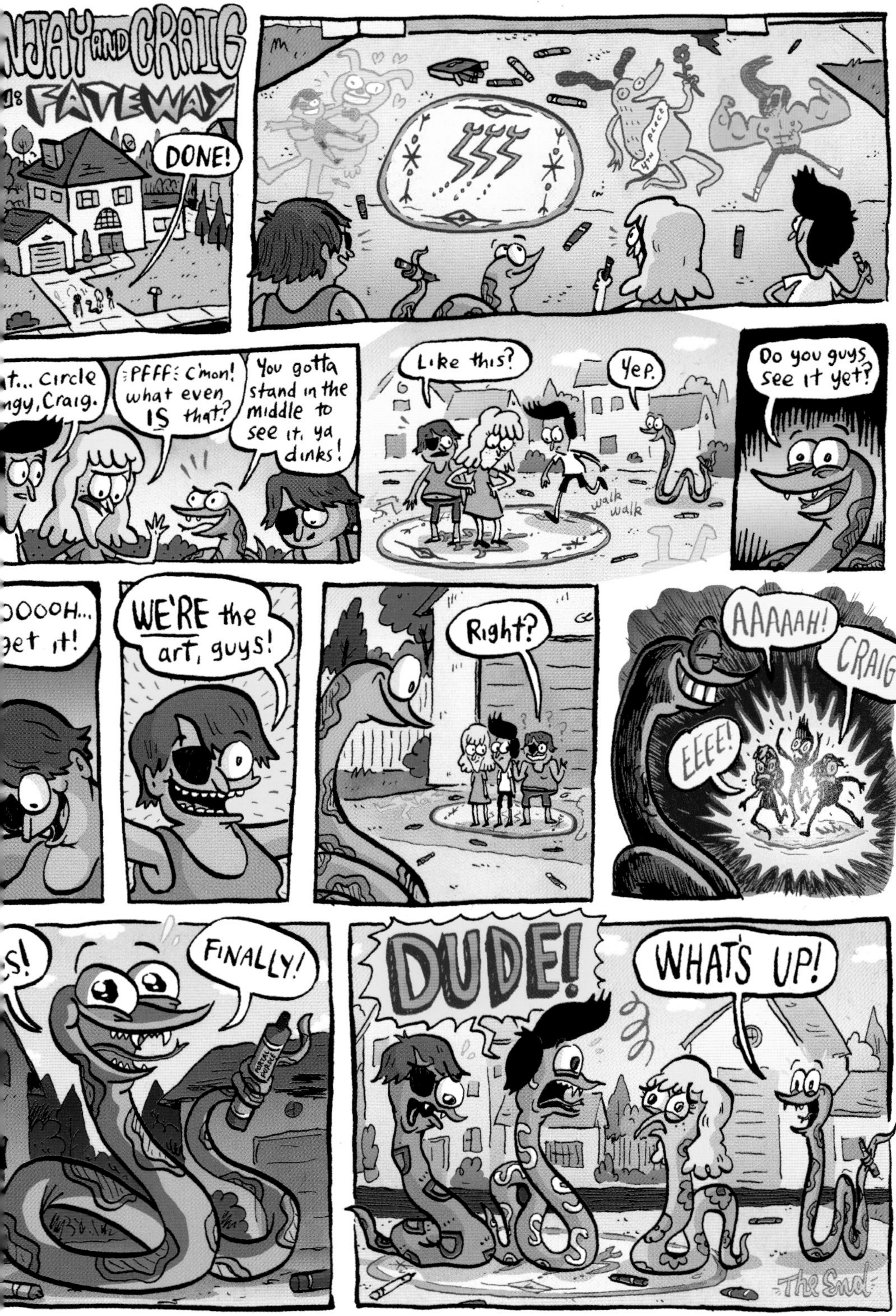

NJAY AND CRAIG
FATEWAY
DONE!
t... circle
ngy, Craig.
PFFF! C'mon! what even IS that?
You gotta stand in the middle to see it, ya dinks!
Like this?
Yep.
walk
walk
Do you guys see it yet?
OOOOH...
get it!
WE'RE the art, guys!
Right?
AAAAAH!
CRAIG!
EEEE!
S!
FINALLY!
DUDE!
WHAT'S UP!
The End

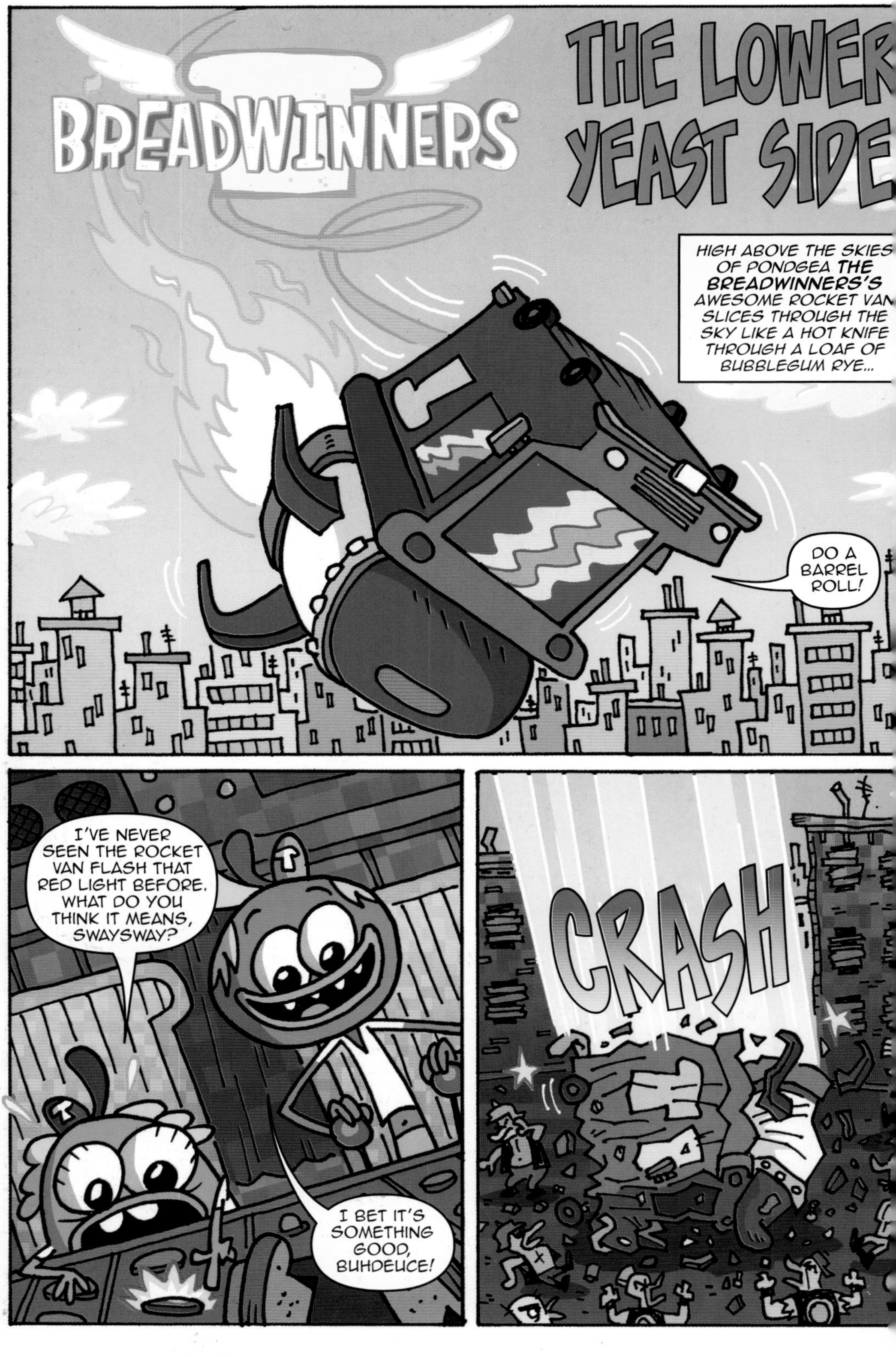
BREADWINNERS
THE LOWER YEAST SIDE
HIGH ABOVE THE SKIES OF PONDGEA THE BREADWINNERS'S AWESOME ROCKET VAN SLICES THROUGH THE SKY LIKE A HOT KNIFE THROUGH A LOAF OF BUBBLEGUM RYE...
DO A BARREL ROLL!
I'VE NEVER SEEN THE ROCKET VAN FLASH THAT RED LIGHT BEFORE. WHAT DO YOU THINK IT MEANS, SWAYSWAY?
I BET IT'S SOMETHING GOOD, BUHDEUCE!
CRASH

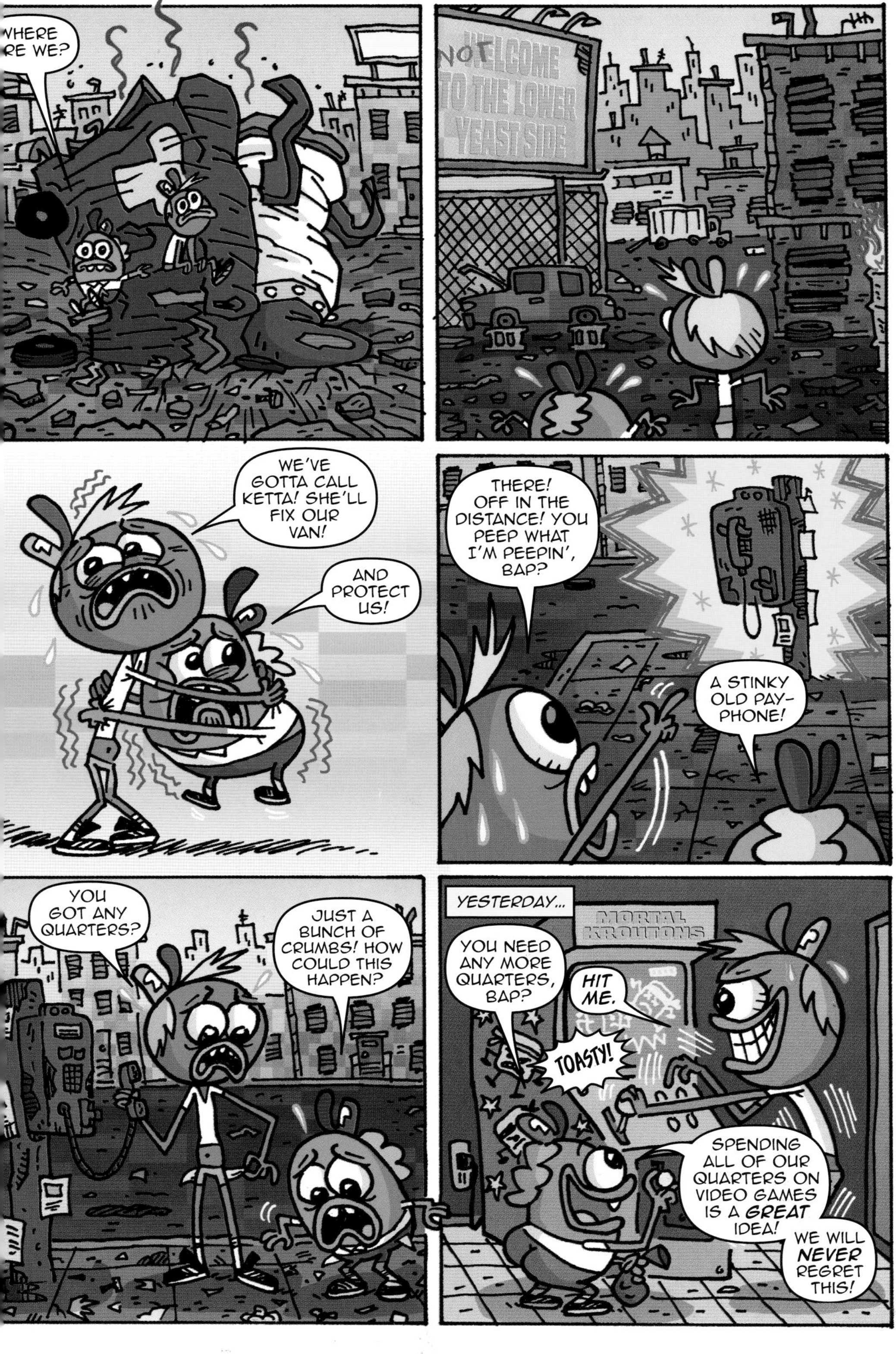

WHERE
RE WE?
NOT WELCOME TO THE LOWER YEAST SIDE
WE'VE GOTTA CALL KETTA! SHE'LL FIX OUR VAN!
AND PROTECT US!
THERE! OFF IN THE DISTANCE! YOU PEEP WHAT I'M PEEPIN', BAP?
A STINKY OLD PAY-PHONE!
YOU GOT ANY QUARTERS?
JUST A BUNCH OF CRUMBS! HOW COULD THIS HAPPEN?
YESTERDAY...
MORTAL KROUTONS
YOU NEED ANY MORE QUARTERS, BAP?
HIT ME.
TOASTY!
SPENDING ALL OF OUR QUARTERS ON VIDEO GAMES IS A *GREAT* IDEA!
WE WILL *NEVER* REGRET THIS!

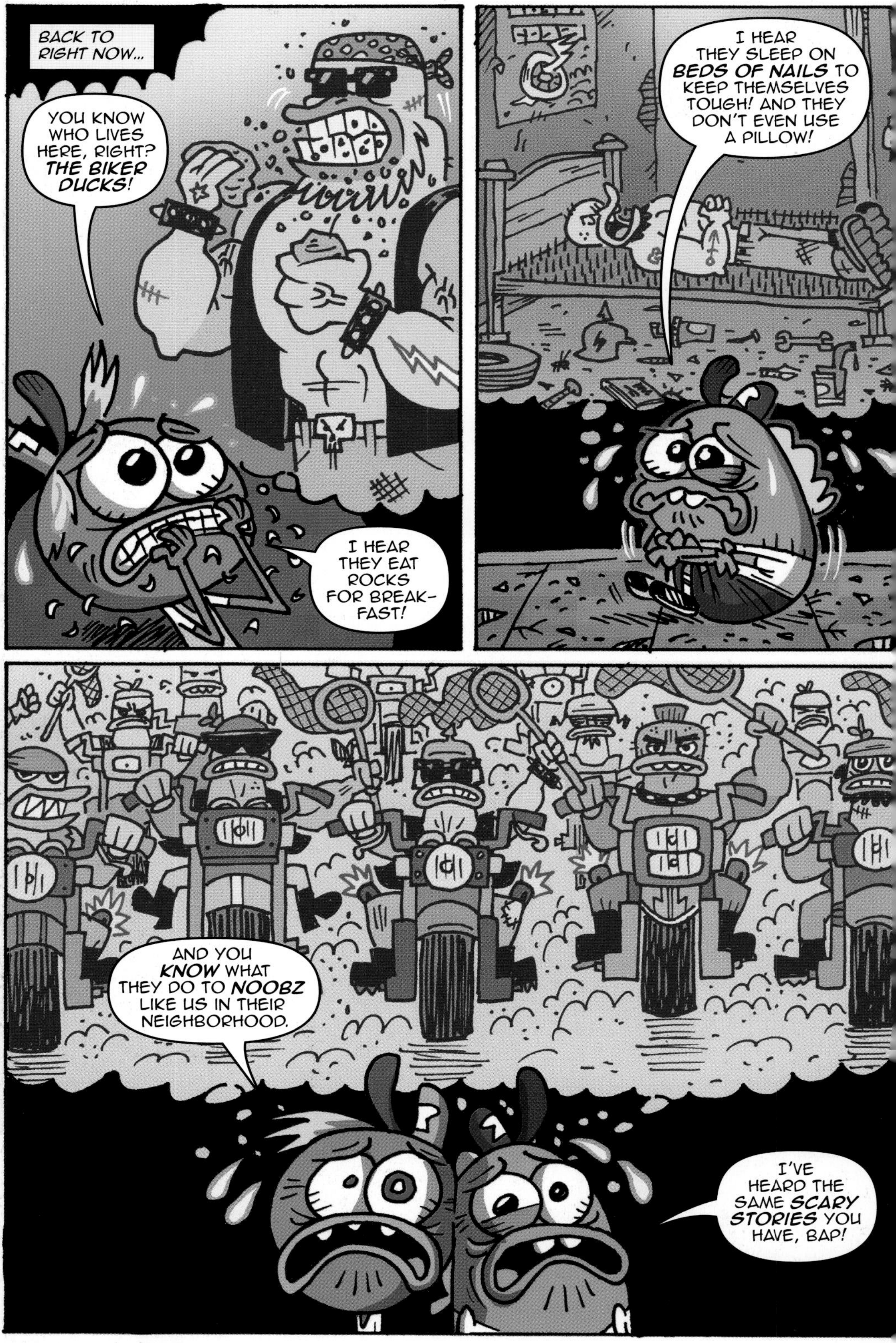
BACK TO RIGHT NOW...
YOU KNOW WHO LIVES HERE, RIGHT? THE BIKER DUCKS!
I HEAR THEY EAT ROCKS FOR BREAK-FAST!
I HEAR THEY SLEEP ON BEDS OF NAILS TO KEEP THEMSELVES TOUGH! AND THEY DON'T EVEN USE A PILLOW!
AND YOU KNOW WHAT THEY DO TO NOOBZ LIKE US IN THEIR NEIGHBORHOOD.
I'VE HEARD THE SAME SCARY STORIES YOU HAVE, BAP!

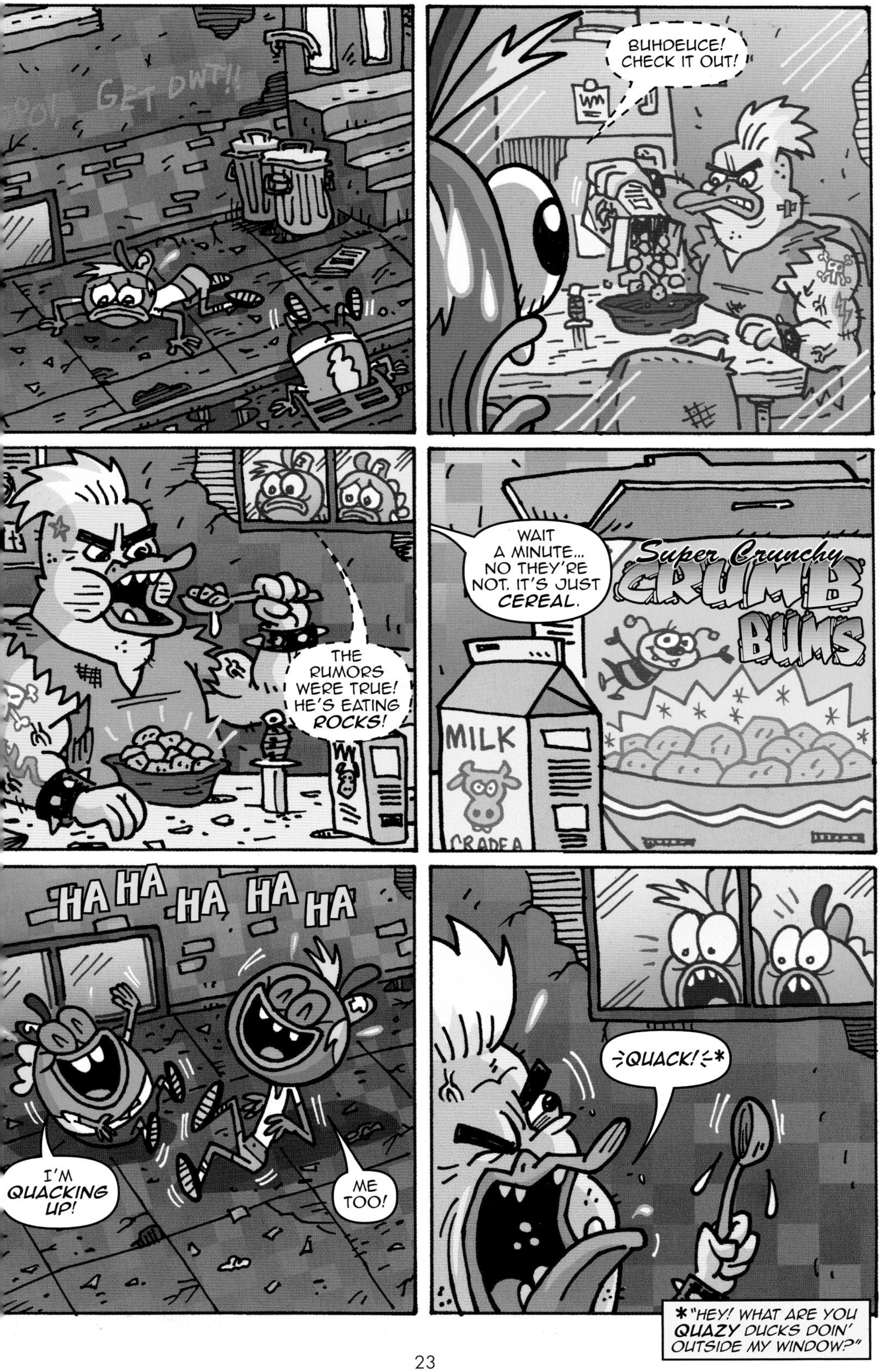
GET OWT!!
BUHDEUCE! CHECK IT OUT!
THE RUMORS WERE TRUE! HE'S EATING ROCKS!
WAIT A MINUTE... NO THEY'RE NOT. IT'S JUST CEREAL.
Super Crunchy CRUMB BUMS
MILK
HA HA HA HA HA
I'M QUACKING UP!
ME TOO!
QUACK!*
*"HEY! WHAT ARE YOU QUAZY DUCKS DOIN' OUTSIDE MY WINDOW?"

THEY MAY NOT EAT ROCKS FOR BREAKFAST, BUT THESE BIKER DUCKS ARE STILL PRETTY TOUGH!

AHHH!

LOOK!

I'M A LITTLE BUSY HERE, 'DEUCE!

⇒QUACK!⇐ *

* "I CAN'T WAIT TO TAKE A NAP ON THIS NEW ORTHOPEDIC BED! DOCTOR SAID IT'D CLEAR MY BACK PROBLEMS RIGHT UP!"

WHAT'S SO FUNNY?

I THINK MAYBE THESE GUYS ARE LOT LESS SCARY THAN WE THOUGHT.

YOU BETTER HOPE YOU'RE RIGHT, BAP!

⇒QUACK!⇐

* "I'M GONN NEED SOM BACKUP, BOY CAUGHT A COUPLE OF NOOBZ TRY TO SNEAK IN TOWN WITHO MEETING TH WELCOMIN COMMITTE

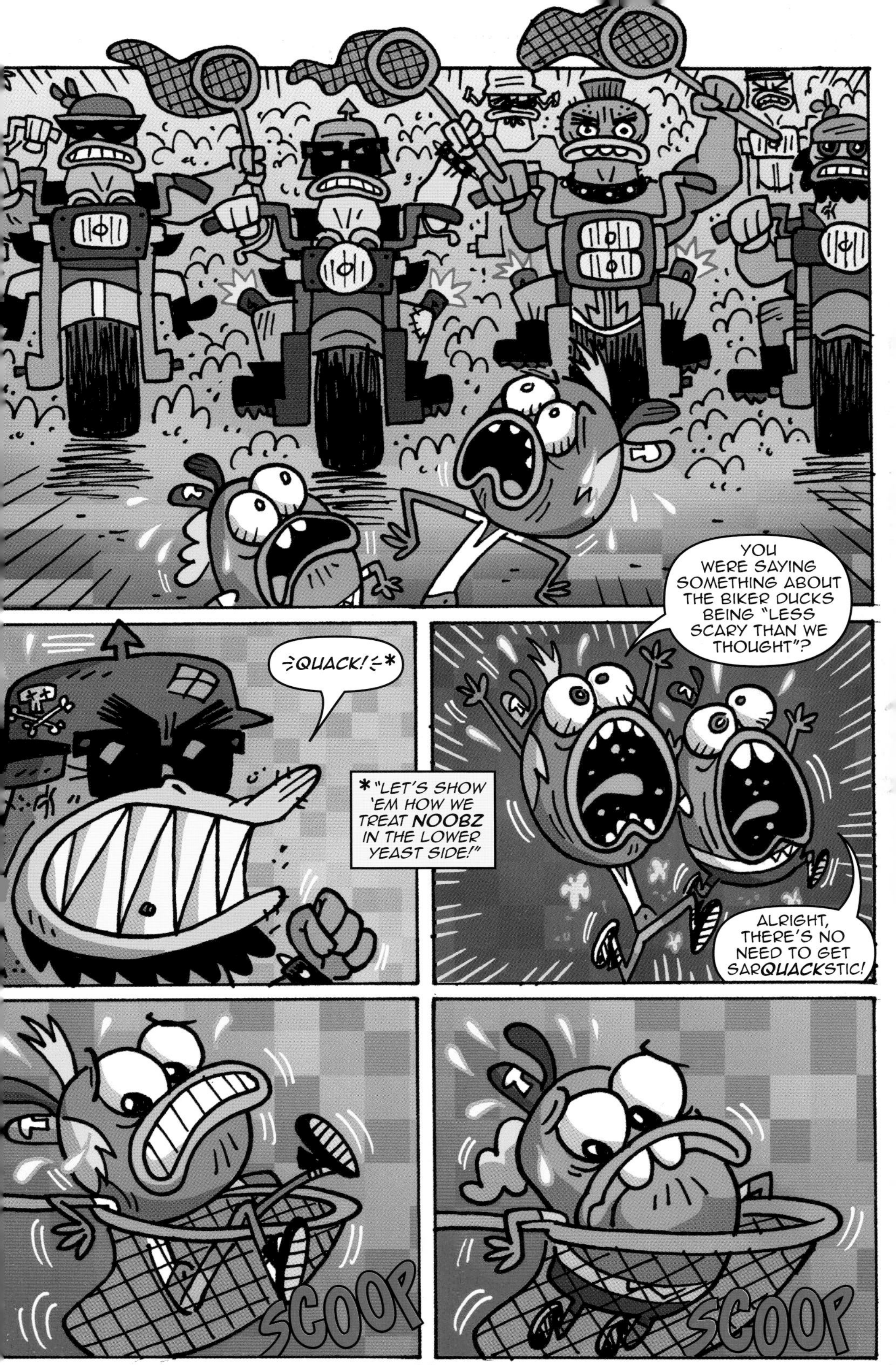
YOU WERE SAYING SOMETHING ABOUT THE BIKER DUCKS BEING "LESS SCARY THAN WE THOUGHT"?
QUACK! *
* "LET'S SHOW 'EM HOW WE TREAT NOOBZ IN THE LOWER YEAST SIDE!"
ALRIGHT, THERE'S NO NEED TO GET SARQUACKSTIC!
SCOOP
SCOOP

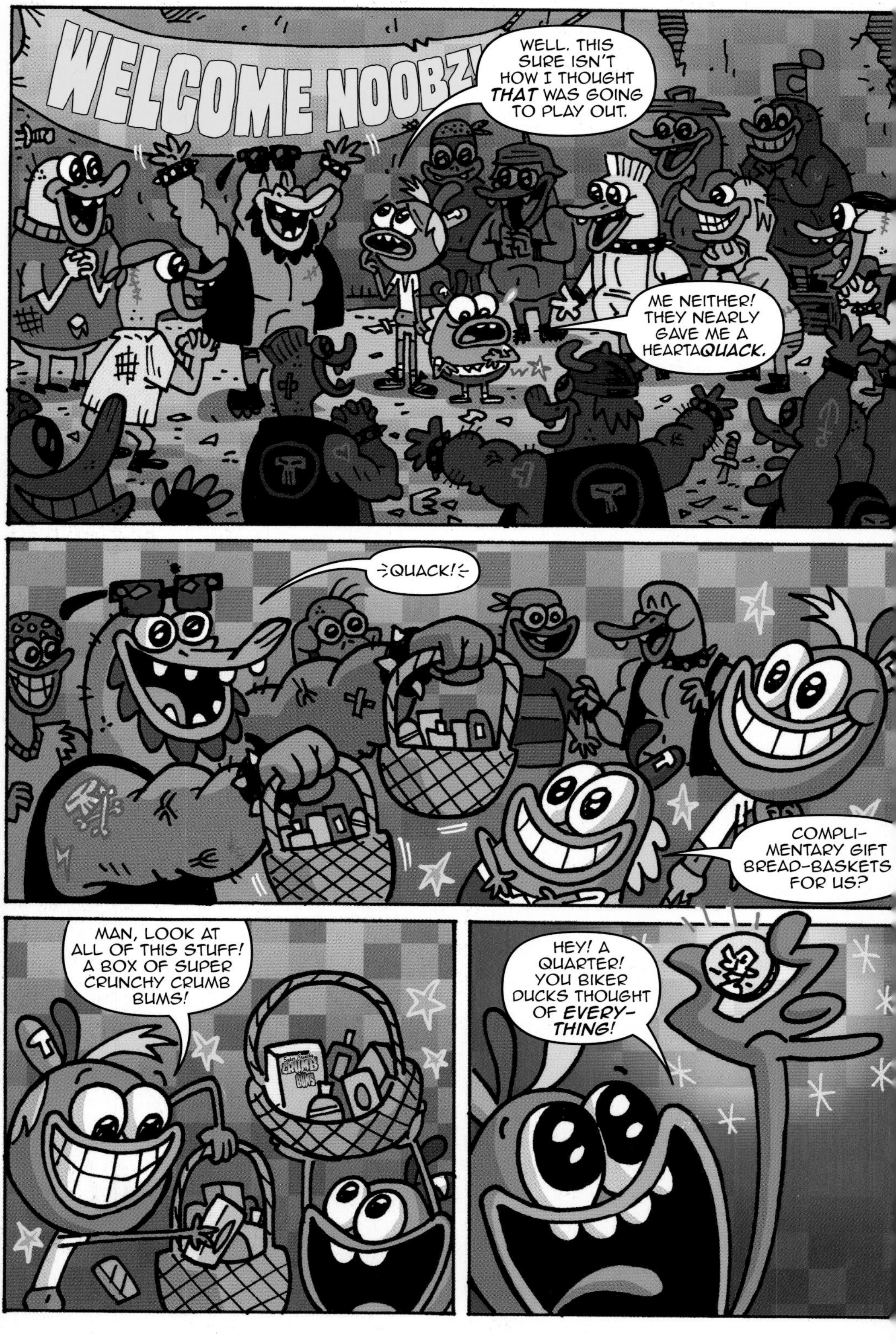
WELCOME NOOBZ!
WELL, THIS SURE ISN'T HOW I THOUGHT THAT WAS GOING TO PLAY OUT.
ME NEITHER! THEY NEARLY GAVE ME A HEARTAQUACK.
QUACK!
COMPLIMENTARY GIFT BREAD-BASKETS FOR US?
MAN, LOOK AT ALL OF THIS STUFF! A BOX OF SUPER CRUNCHY CRUMB BUMS!
Super Crunchy CRUMB BUMS
HEY! A QUARTER! YOU BIKER DUCKS THOUGHT OF EVERYTHING!

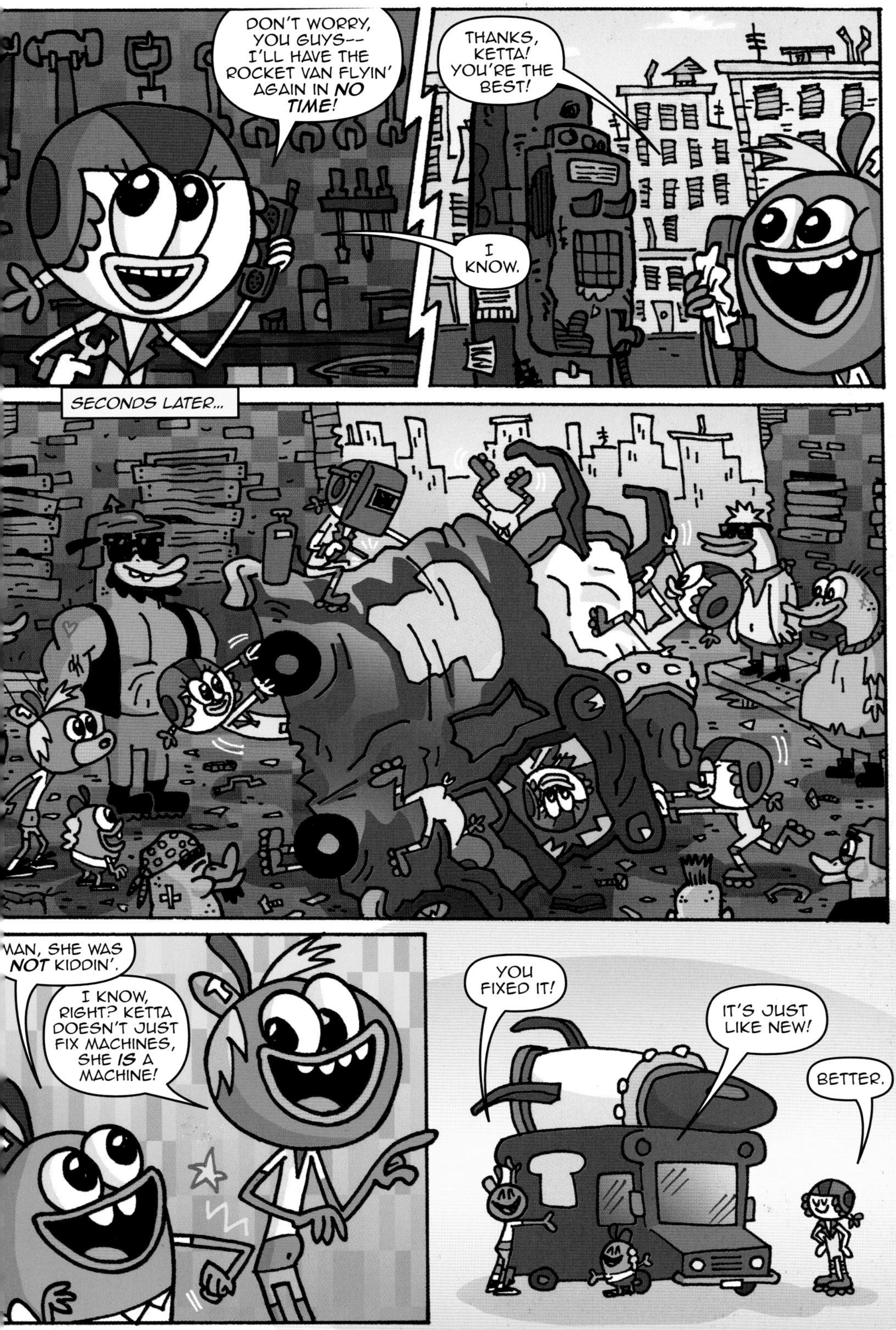
DON'T WORRY, YOU GUYS-- I'LL HAVE THE ROCKET VAN FLYIN' AGAIN IN NO TIME!
THANKS, KETTA! YOU'RE THE BEST!
I KNOW.
SECONDS LATER...
MAN, SHE WAS NOT KIDDIN'.
I KNOW, RIGHT? KETTA DOESN'T JUST FIX MACHINES, SHE IS A MACHINE!
YOU FIXED IT!
IT'S JUST LIKE NEW!
BETTER.

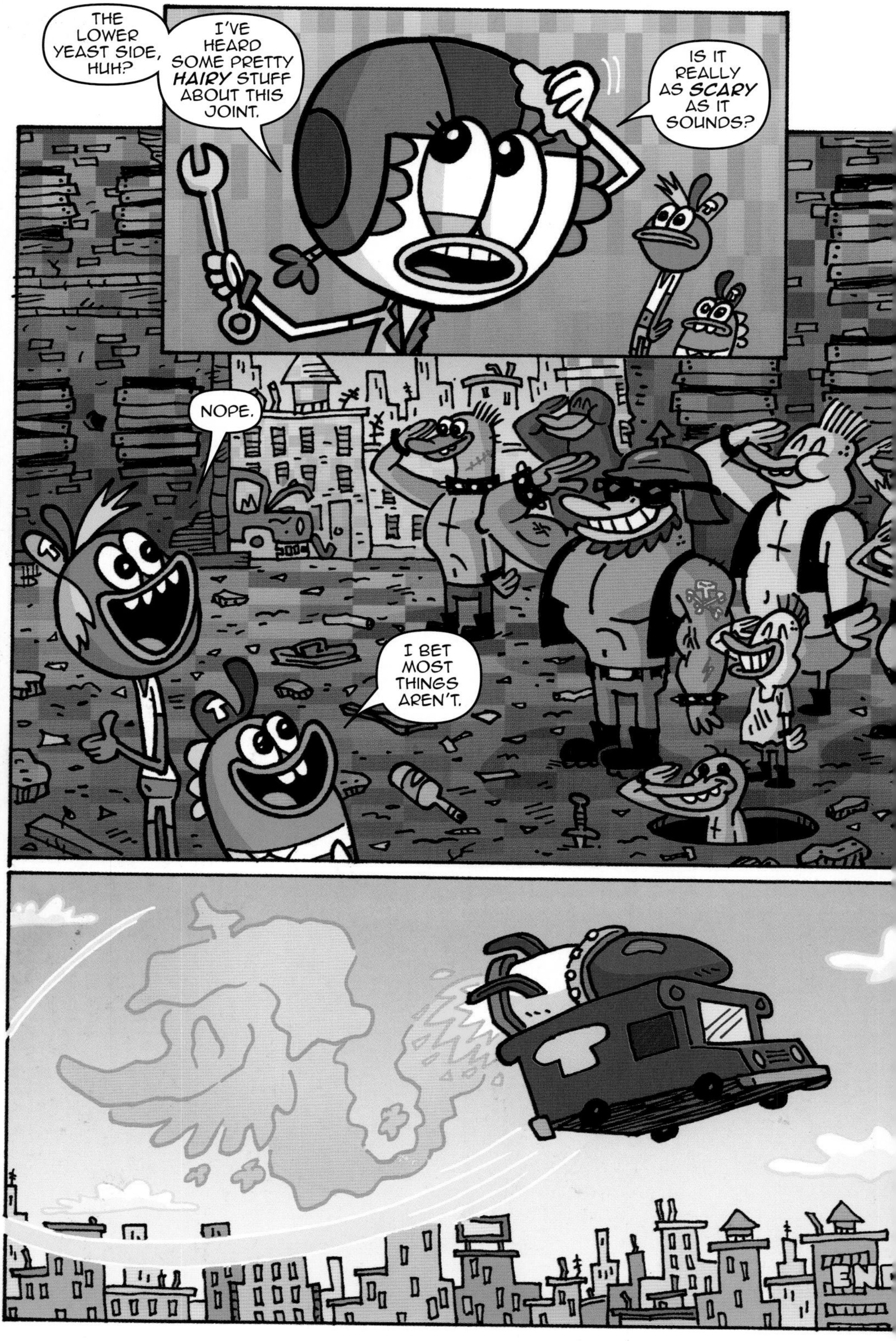
THE LOWER YEAST SIDE, HUH?
I'VE HEARD SOME PRETTY **HAIRY** STUFF ABOUT THIS JOINT.
IS IT REALLY AS **SCARY** AS IT SOUNDS?
NOPE.
I BET MOST THINGS AREN'T.
END

FOO FACTS #81- FIRE

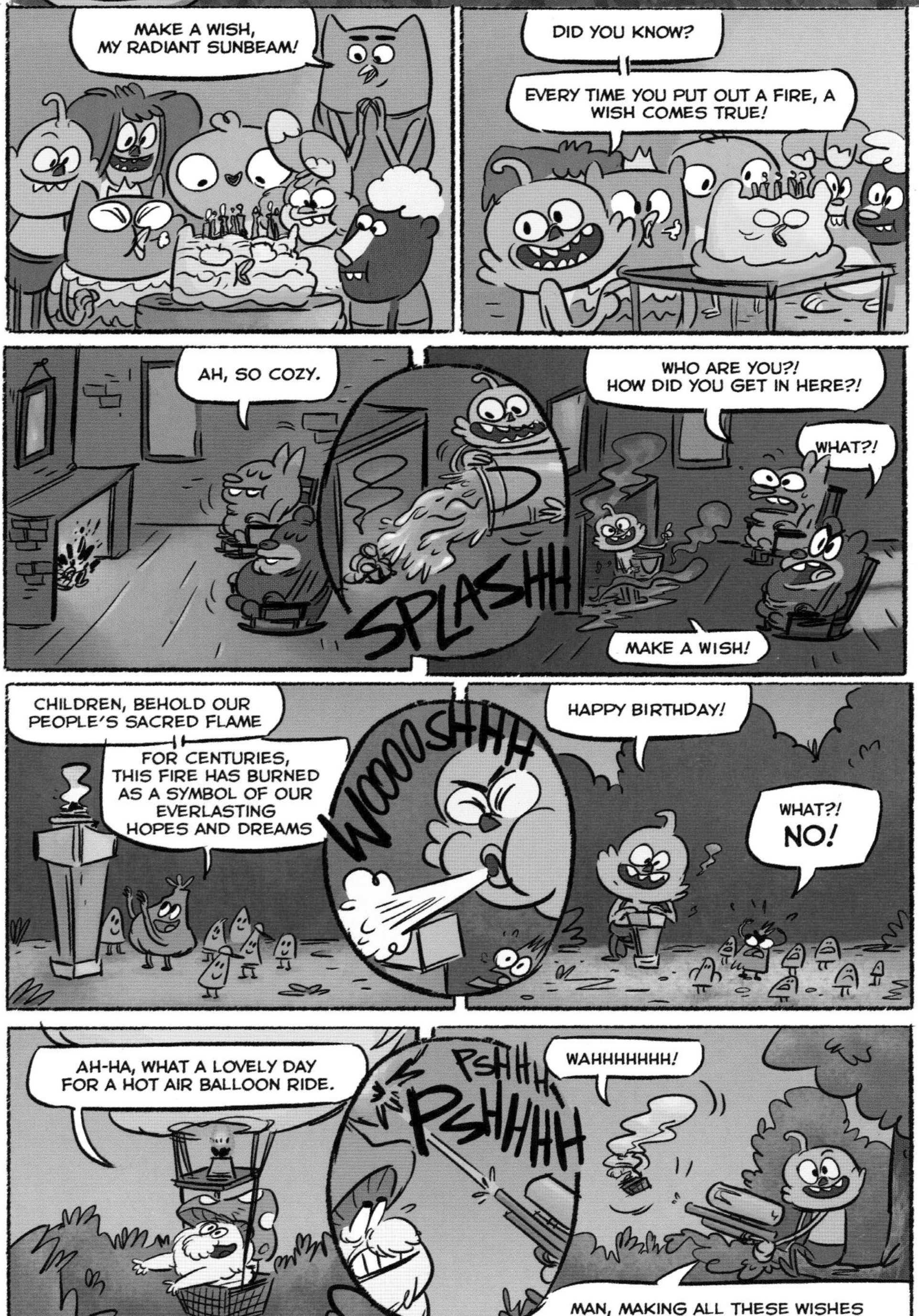

MAKE A WISH, MY RADIANT SUNBEAM!
DID YOU KNOW?
EVERY TIME YOU PUT OUT A FIRE, A WISH COMES TRUE!
AH, SO COZY.
SPLASHH
WHO ARE YOU?! HOW DID YOU GET IN HERE?!
WHAT?!
MAKE A WISH!
CHILDREN, BEHOLD OUR PEOPLE'S SACRED FLAME
FOR CENTURIES, THIS FIRE HAS BURNED AS A SYMBOL OF OUR EVERLASTING HOPES AND DREAMS
WOOOOSHHH
HAPPY BIRTHDAY!
WHAT?! NO!
AH-HA, WHAT A LOVELY DAY FOR A HOT AIR BALLOON RIDE.
PSHHH
PSHHHH
WAHHHHHHH!
MAN, MAKING ALL THESE WISHES COME TRUE IS LIKE A WISH COME TRUE!
SCHUSTER

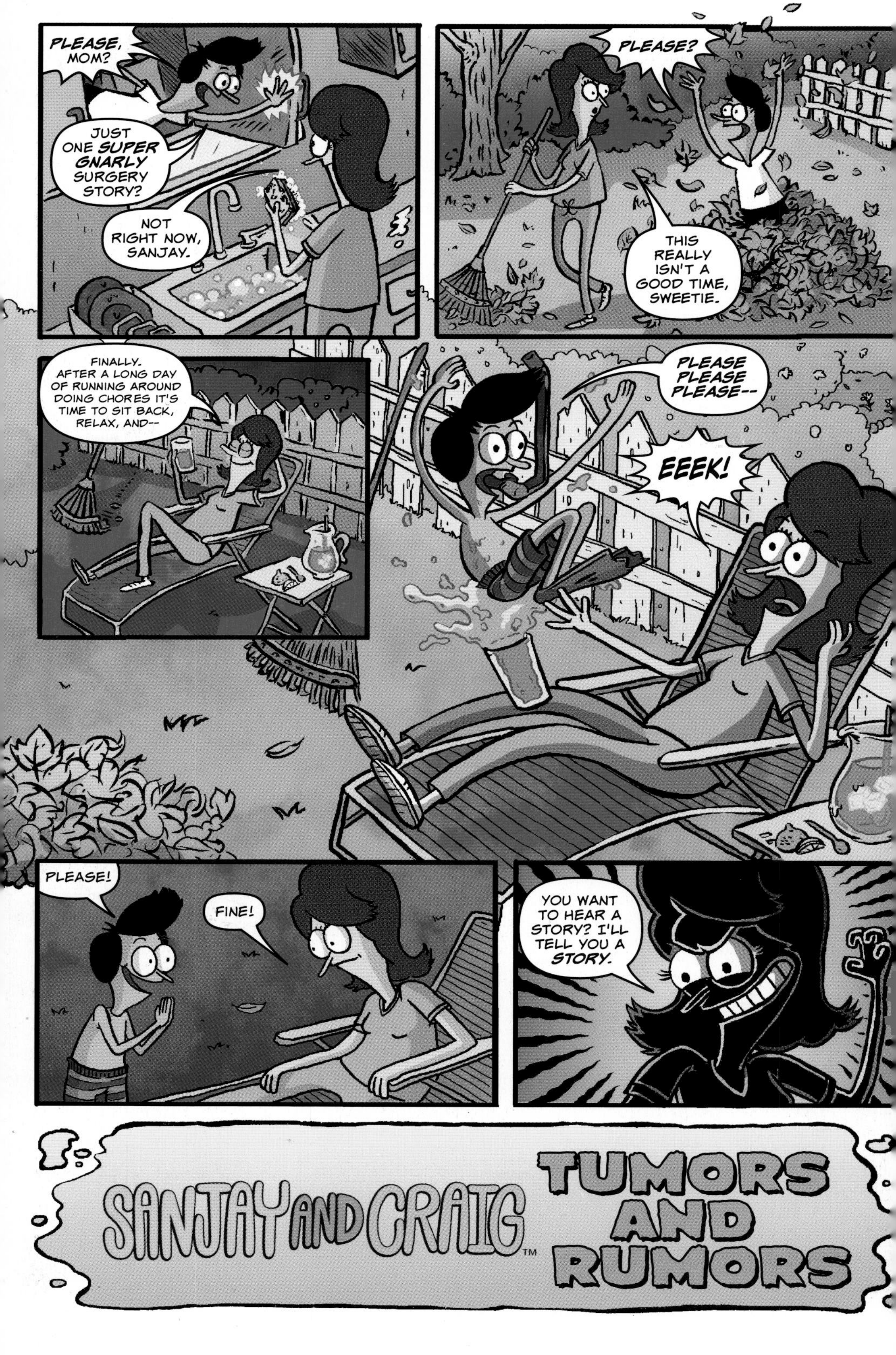

PLEASE, MOM?
JUST ONE SUPER GNARLY SURGERY STORY?
NOT RIGHT NOW, SANJAY.
PLEASE?
THIS REALLY ISN'T A GOOD TIME, SWEETIE.
FINALLY. AFTER A LONG DAY OF RUNNING AROUND DOING CHORES IT'S TIME TO SIT BACK, RELAX, AND--
PLEASE PLEASE PLEASE--
EEEK!
PLEASE!
FINE!
YOU WANT TO HEAR A STORY? I'LL TELL YOU A STORY.
SANJAY AND CRAIG™
TUMORS AND RUMORS

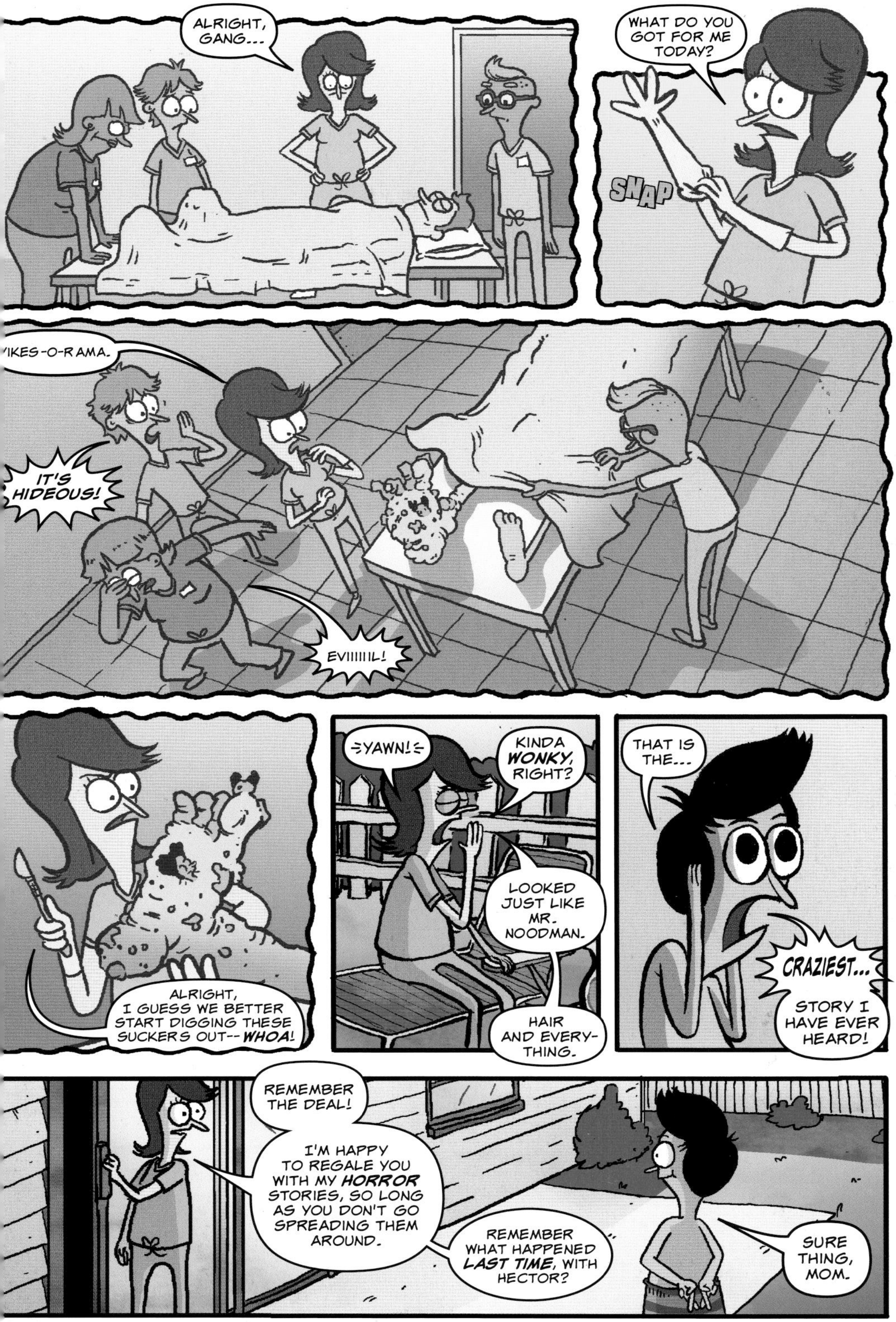
ALRIGHT, GANG...
WHAT DO YOU GOT FOR ME TODAY?
SNAP
YIKES-O-RAMA.
IT'S HIDEOUS!
EVIIIIIIL!
ALRIGHT, I GUESS WE BETTER START DIGGING THESE SUCKERS OUT--WHOA!
YAWN!
KINDA WONKY, RIGHT?
LOOKED JUST LIKE MR. NOODMAN.
HAIR AND EVERY-THING.
THAT IS THE...
CRAZIEST...
STORY I HAVE EVER HEARD!
REMEMBER THE DEAL!
I'M HAPPY TO REGALE YOU WITH MY HORROR STORIES, SO LONG AS YOU DON'T GO SPREADING THEM AROUND.
REMEMBER WHAT HAPPENED LAST TIME, WITH HECTOR?
SURE THING, MOM.

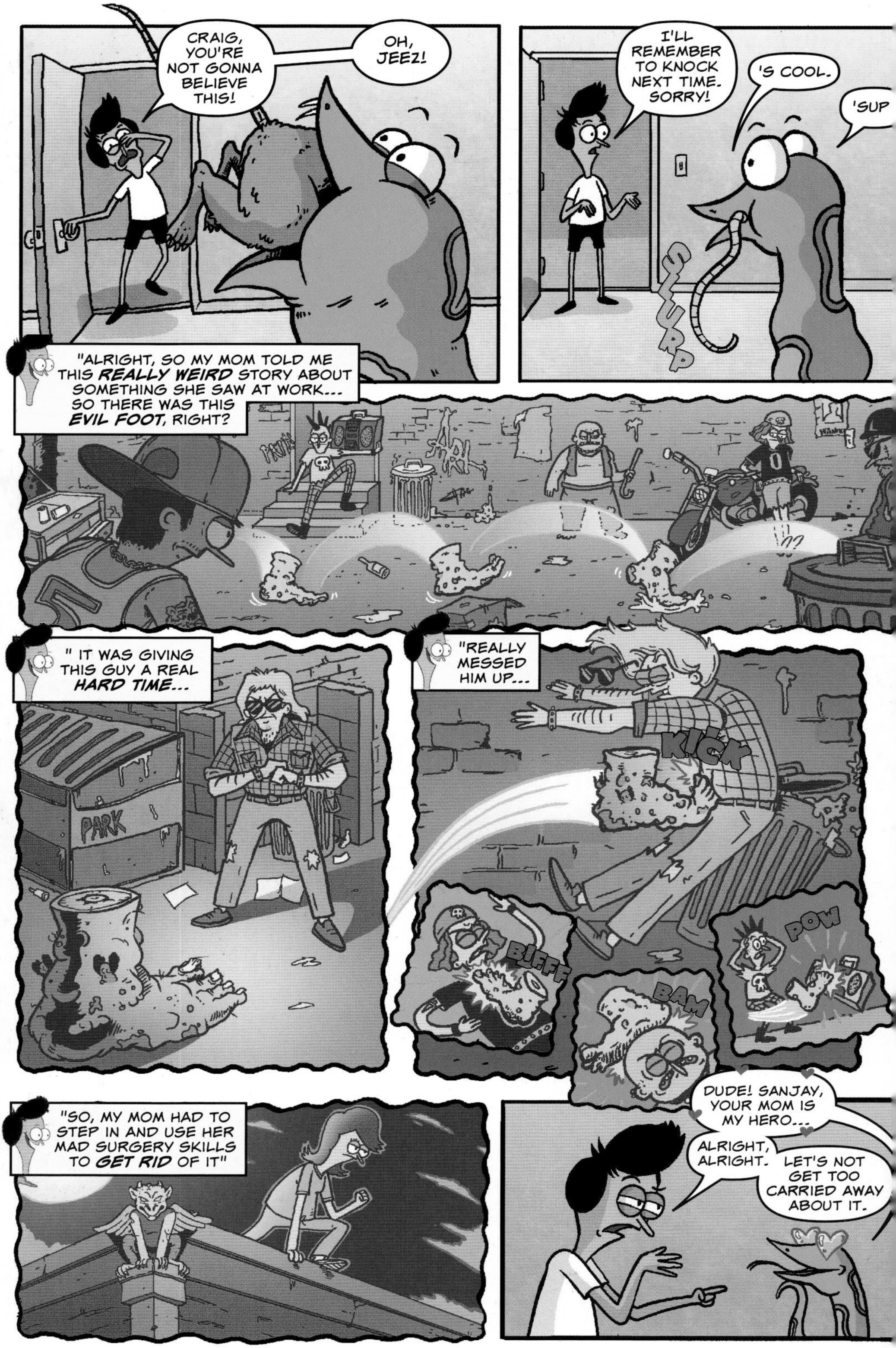
CRAIG, YOU'RE NOT GONNA BELIEVE THIS!
OH, JEEZ!
I'LL REMEMBER TO KNOCK NEXT TIME. SORRY!
'S COOL.
'SUP
SLURP
"ALRIGHT, SO MY MOM TOLD ME THIS REALLY WEIRD STORY ABOUT SOMETHING SHE SAW AT WORK... SO THERE WAS THIS EVIL FOOT, RIGHT?
" IT WAS GIVING THIS GUY A REAL HARD TIME...
PARK
"REALLY MESSED HIM UP...
KICK
BIFFF
BAM
POW
"SO, MY MOM HAD TO STEP IN AND USE HER MAD SURGERY SKILLS TO GET RID OF IT"
DUDE! SANJAY, YOUR MOM IS MY HERO...
ALRIGHT, ALRIGHT.
LET'S NOT GET TOO CARRIED AWAY ABOUT IT.

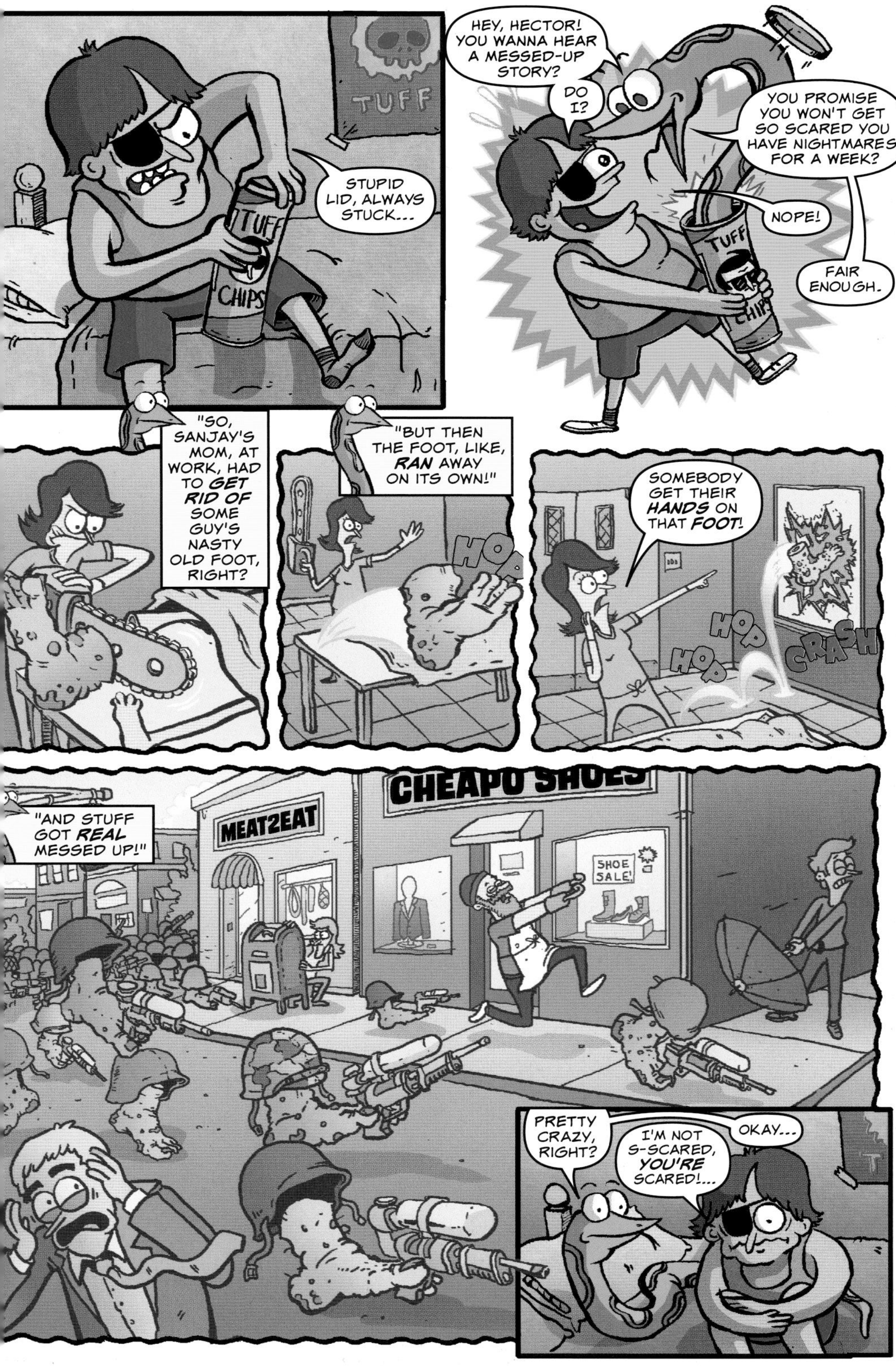
TUFF
STUPID LID, ALWAYS STUCK...
TUFF CHIPS
HEY, HECTOR! YOU WANNA HEAR A MESSED-UP STORY?
DO I?
YOU PROMISE YOU WON'T GET SO SCARED YOU HAVE NIGHTMARES FOR A WEEK?
NOPE!
FAIR ENOUGH.
"SO, SANJAY'S MOM, AT WORK, HAD TO GET RID OF SOME GUY'S NASTY OLD FOOT, RIGHT?
"BUT THEN THE FOOT, LIKE, RAN AWAY ON ITS OWN!"
HOP
SOMEBODY GET THEIR HANDS ON THAT FOOT!
HOP
HOP
CRASH
"AND STUFF GOT REAL MESSED UP!"
CHEAPO SHOES
MEAT2EAT
SHOE SALE!
PRETTY CRAZY, RIGHT?
I'M NOT S-SCARED, YOU'RE SCARED!...
OKAY...

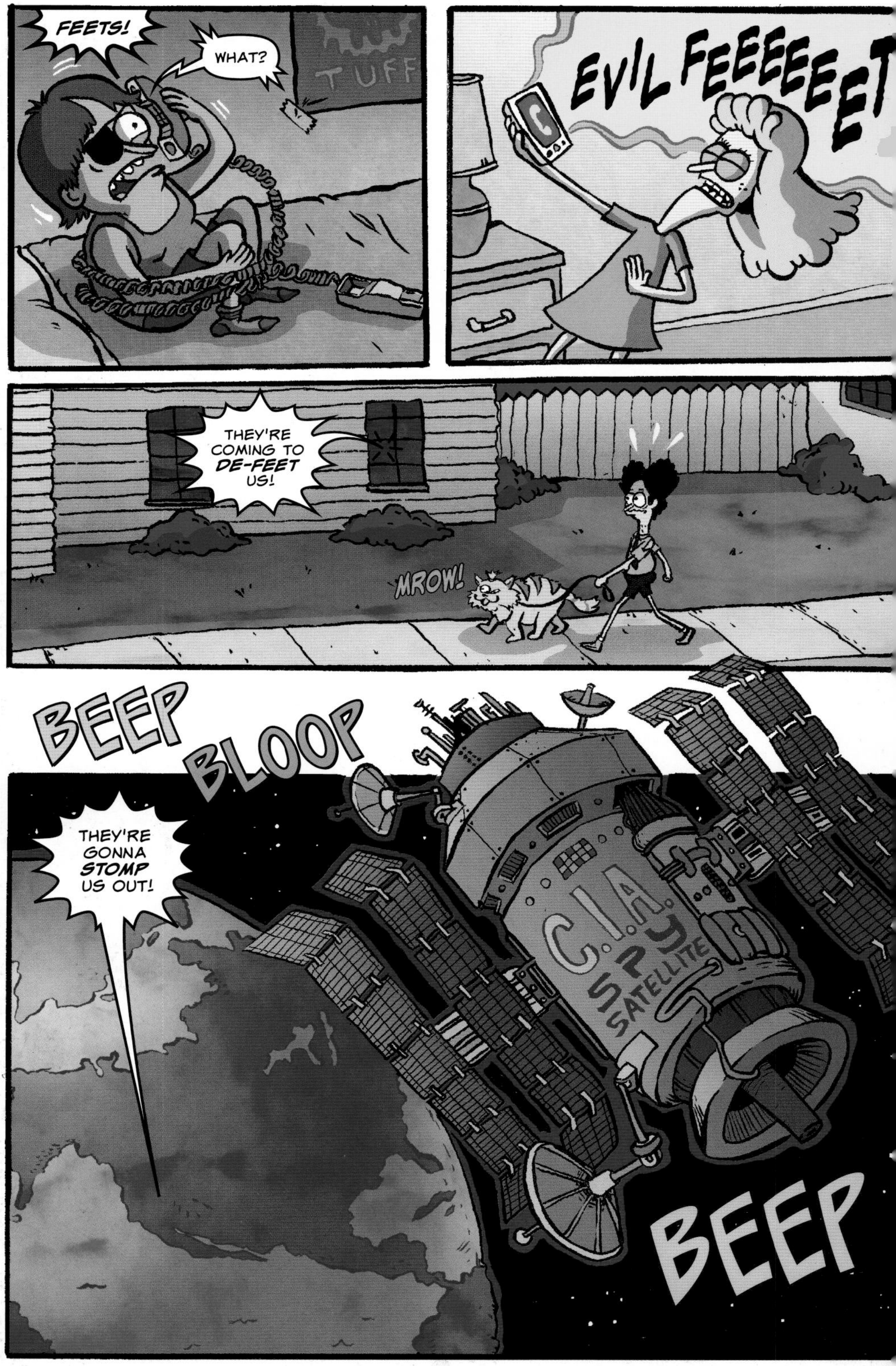
FEETS!
WHAT?
TUFF
EVIL FEEEEEEET
THEY'RE COMING TO DE-FEET US!
MROW!
BEEP
BLOOP
THEY'RE GONNA STOMP US OUT!
C.I.A. SPY SATELLITE
BEEP

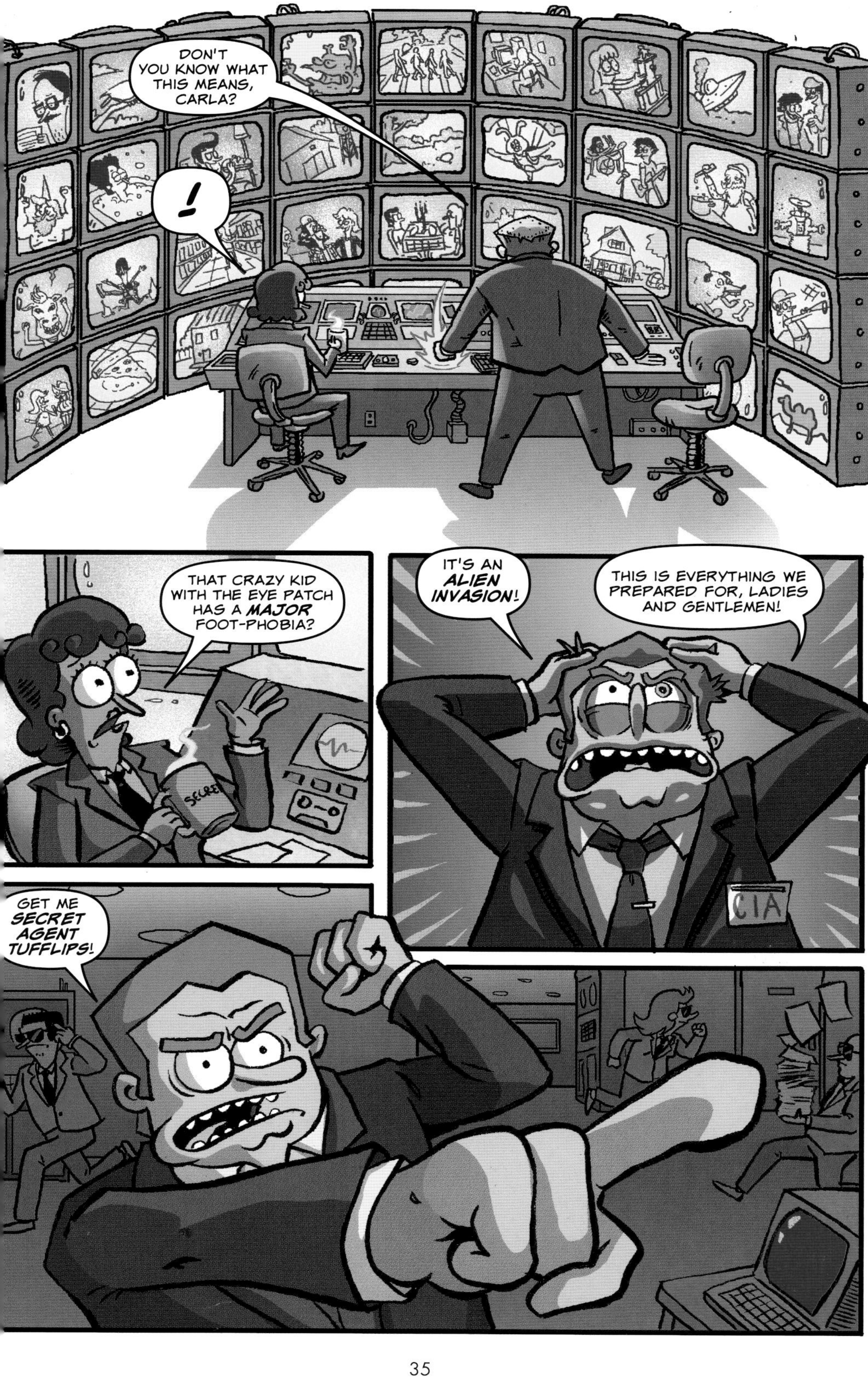
DON'T YOU KNOW WHAT THIS MEANS, CARLA?
!
THAT CRAZY KID WITH THE EYE PATCH HAS A MAJOR FOOT-PHOBIA?
IT'S AN ALIEN INVASION!
THIS IS EVERYTHING WE PREPARED FOR, LADIES AND GENTLEMEN!
GET ME SECRET AGENT TUFFLIPS!
CIA

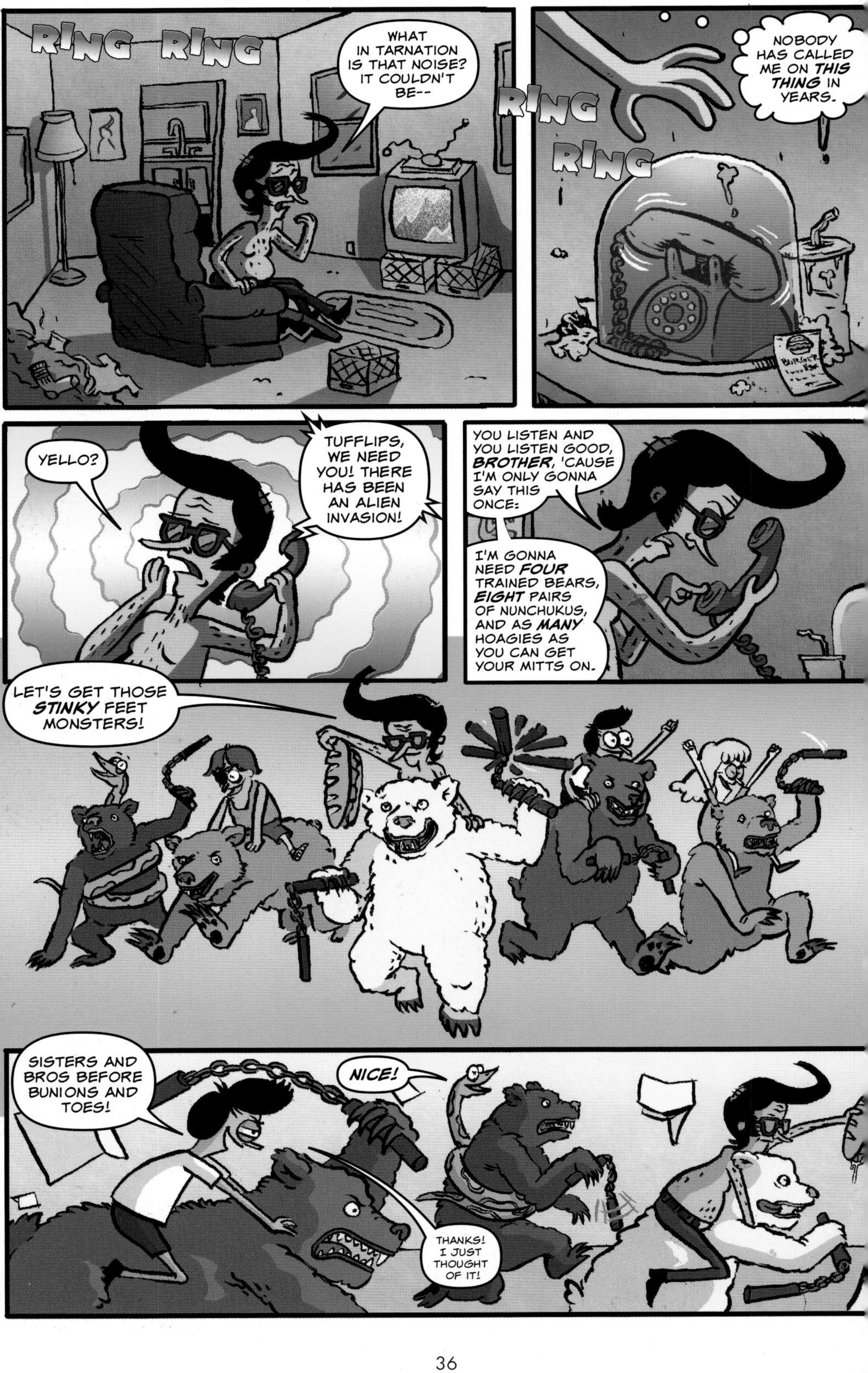
RING RING
WHAT IN TARNATION IS THAT NOISE? IT COULDN'T BE--
RING
RING
NOBODY HAS CALLED ME ON THIS THING IN YEARS.
YELLO?
TUFFLIPS, WE NEED YOU! THERE HAS BEEN AN ALIEN INVASION!
YOU LISTEN AND YOU LISTEN GOOD, BROTHER, 'CAUSE I'M ONLY GONNA SAY THIS ONCE:
I'M GONNA NEED FOUR TRAINED BEARS, EIGHT PAIRS OF NUNCHUKUS, AND AS MANY HOAGIES AS YOU CAN GET YOUR MITTS ON.
LET'S GET THOSE STINKY FEET MONSTERS!
SISTERS AND BROS BEFORE BUNIONS AND TOES!
NICE!
THANKS! I JUST THOUGHT OF IT!

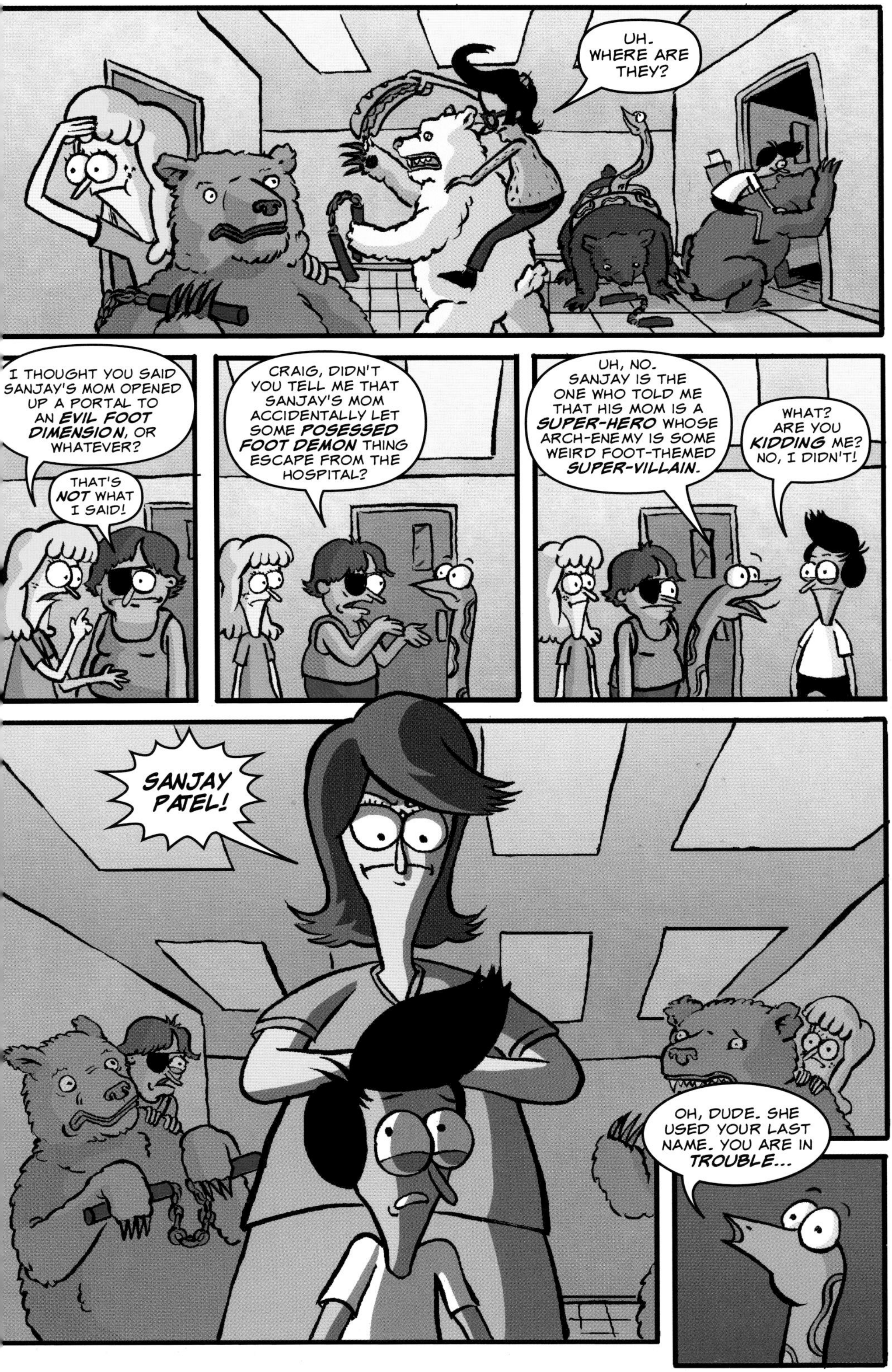
UH. WHERE ARE THEY?
I THOUGHT YOU SAID SANJAY'S MOM OPENED UP A PORTAL TO AN EVIL FOOT DIMENSION, OR WHATEVER?
THAT'S NOT WHAT I SAID!
CRAIG, DIDN'T YOU TELL ME THAT SANJAY'S MOM ACCIDENTALLY LET SOME POSESSED FOOT DEMON THING ESCAPE FROM THE HOSPITAL?
UH, NO. SANJAY IS THE ONE WHO TOLD ME THAT HIS MOM IS A SUPER-HERO WHOSE ARCH-ENEMY IS SOME WEIRD FOOT-THEMED SUPER-VILLAIN.
WHAT? ARE YOU KIDDING ME? NO, I DIDN'T!
SANJAY PATEL!
OH, DUDE. SHE USED YOUR LAST NAME. YOU ARE IN TROUBLE...

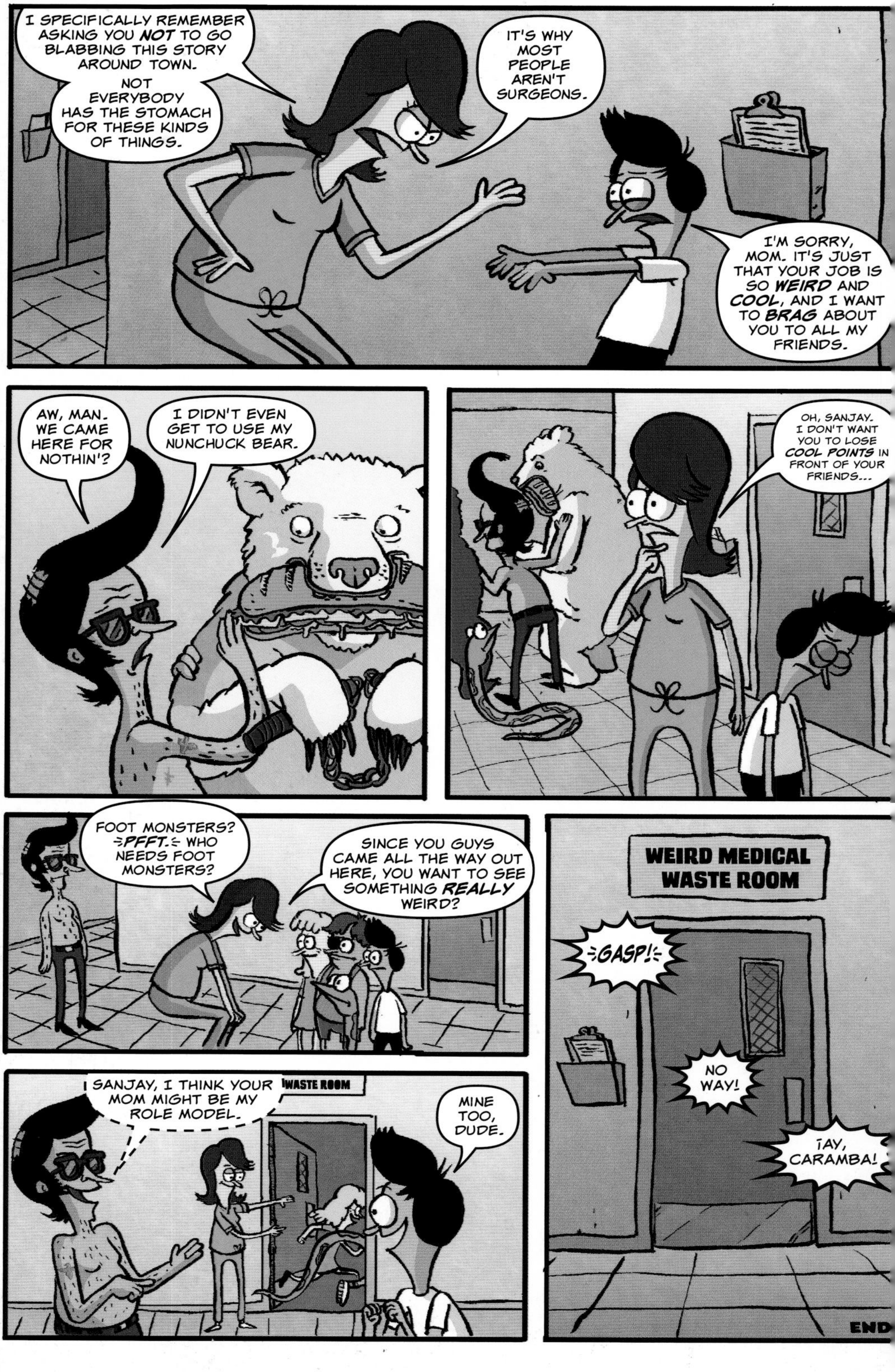
I SPECIFICALLY REMEMBER ASKING YOU NOT TO GO BLABBING THIS STORY AROUND TOWN.
NOT EVERYBODY HAS THE STOMACH FOR THESE KINDS OF THINGS.
IT'S WHY MOST PEOPLE AREN'T SURGEONS.
I'M SORRY, MOM. IT'S JUST THAT YOUR JOB IS SO WEIRD AND COOL, AND I WANT TO BRAG ABOUT YOU TO ALL MY FRIENDS.
AW, MAN. WE CAME HERE FOR NOTHIN'?
I DIDN'T EVEN GET TO USE MY NUNCHUCK BEAR.
OH, SANJAY. I DON'T WANT YOU TO LOSE COOL POINTS IN FRONT OF YOUR FRIENDS...
FOOT MONSTERS? PFFT. WHO NEEDS FOOT MONSTERS?
SINCE YOU GUYS CAME ALL THE WAY OUT HERE, YOU WANT TO SEE SOMETHING REALLY WEIRD?
WEIRD MEDICAL WASTE ROOM
GASP!
NO WAY!
¡AY, CARAMBA!
END
WASTE ROOM
SANJAY, I THINK YOUR MOM MIGHT BE MY ROLE MODEL.
MINE TOO, DUDE.

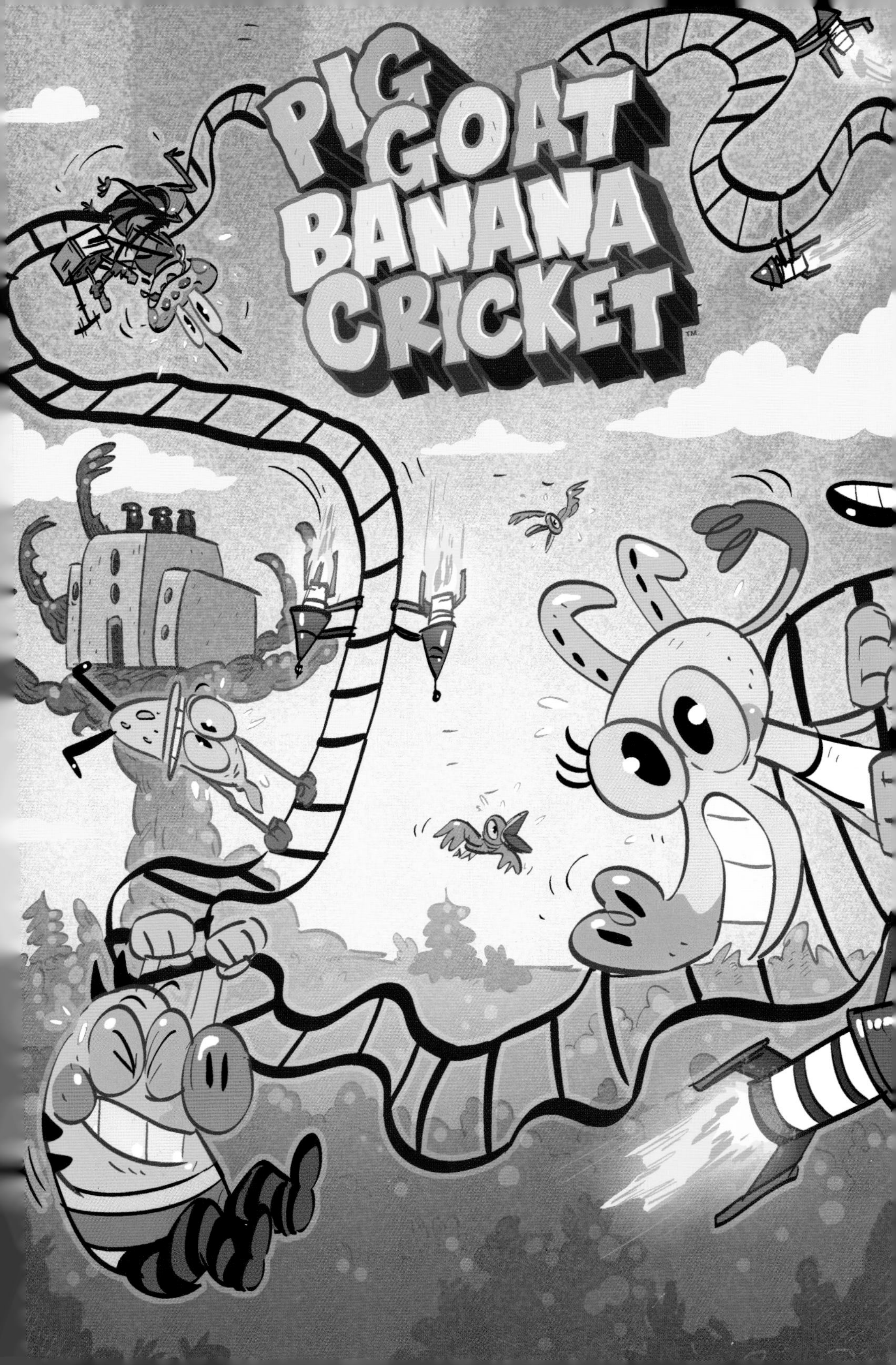
PIG GOAT BANANA CRICKET™

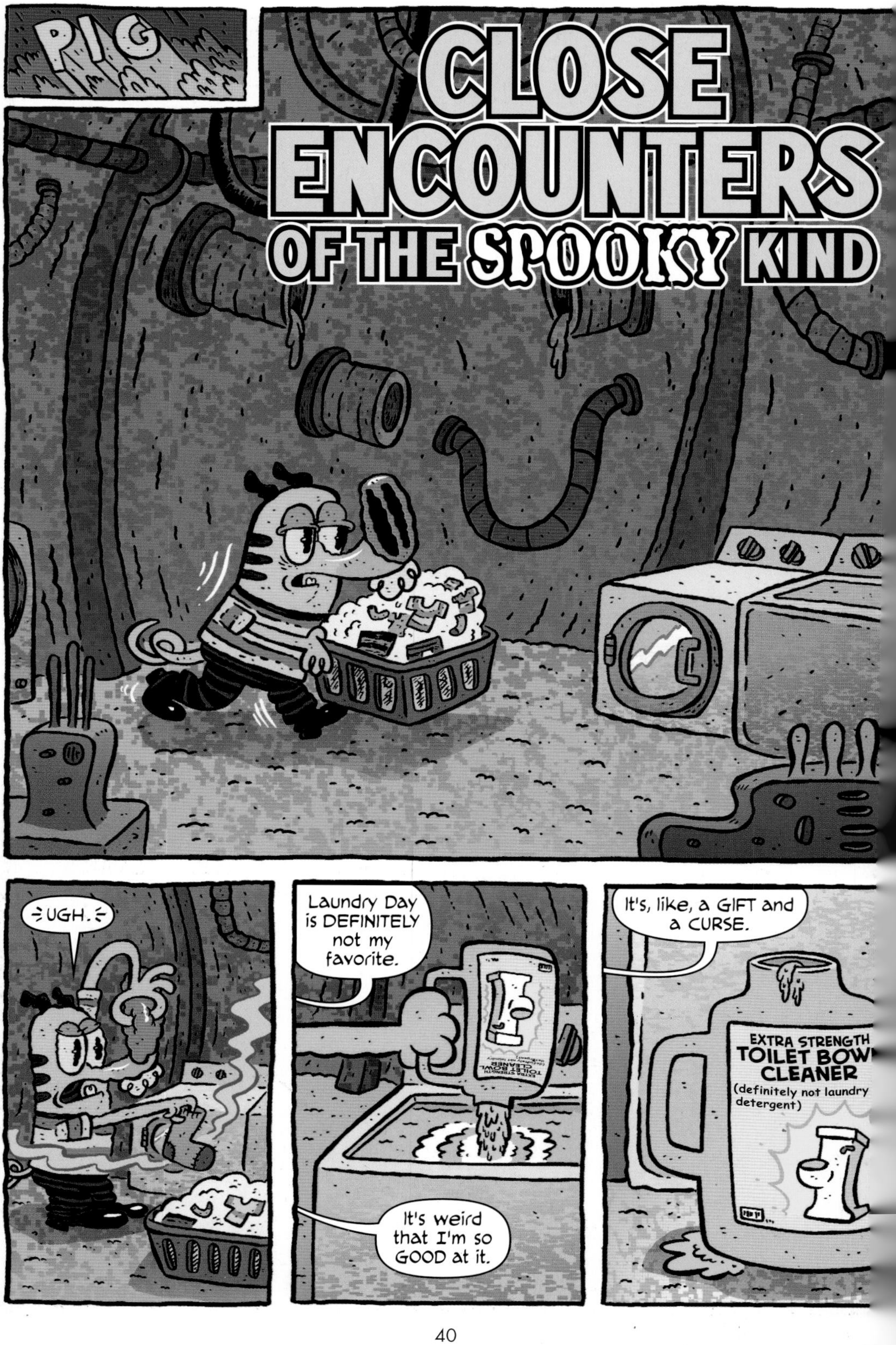
PIG
CLOSE ENCOUNTERS OF THE SPOOKY KIND
UGH.
Laundry Day is DEFINITELY not my favorite.
It's weird that I'm so GOOD at it.
It's, like, a GIFT and a CURSE.
EXTRA STRENGTH
TOILET BOW
CLEANER
(definitely not laundry detergent)

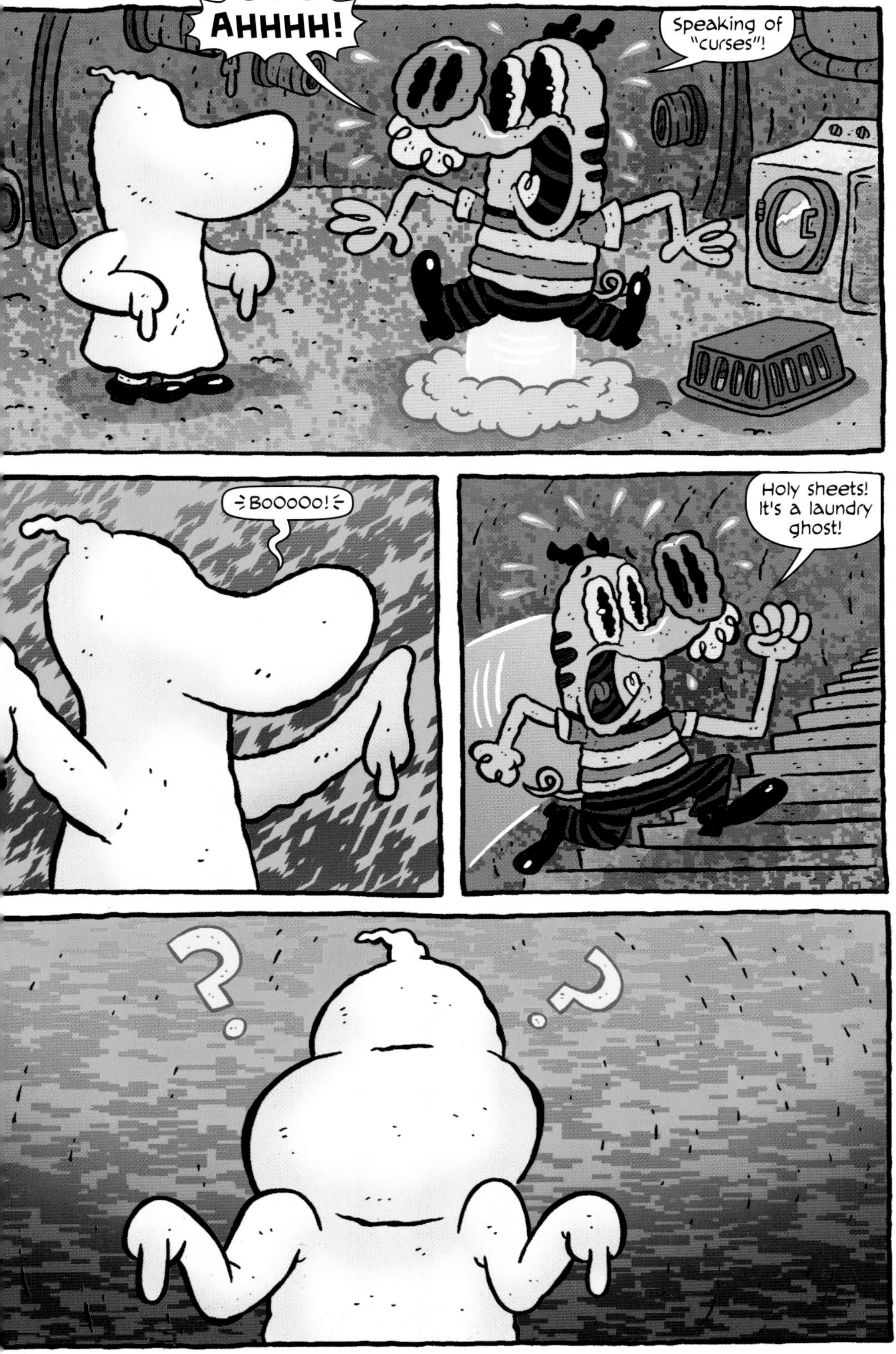
AHHHH!
Speaking of "curses"!
BOOOOO!
Holy sheets! It's a laundry ghost!

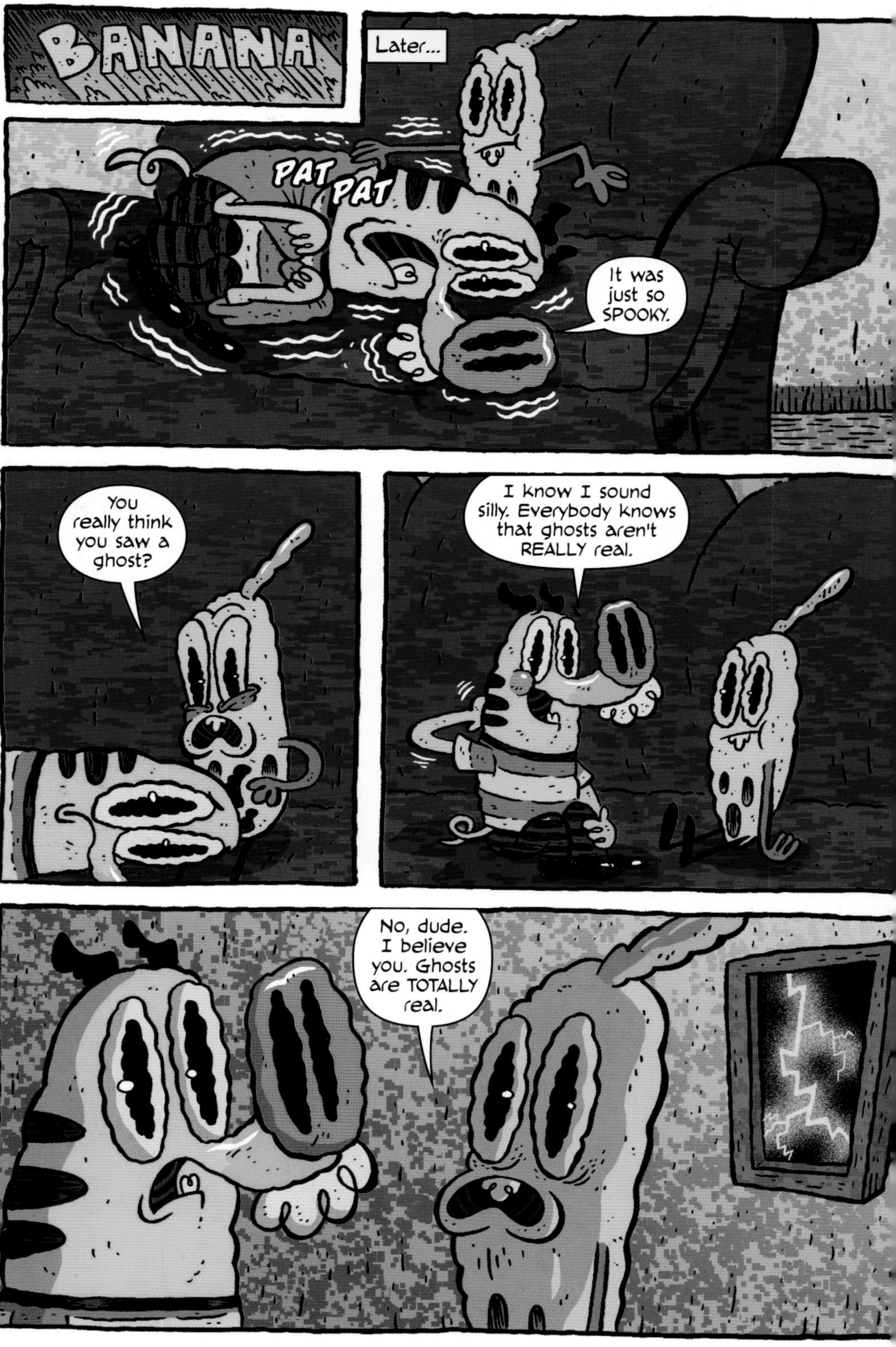
BANANA
Later...
PAT PAT
It was just so SPOOKY.
You really think you saw a ghost?
I know I sound silly. Everybody knows that ghosts aren't REALLY real.
No, dude. I believe you. Ghosts are TOTALLY real.

Y-you m-mean, I didn't just imagine it?

Heck naw, dawg! Ghosts are as real as you or me.

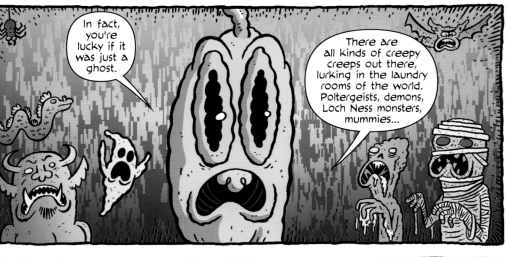

In fact, you're lucky if it was just a ghost.

There are all kinds of creepy creeps out there, lurking in the laundry rooms of the world. Poltergeists, demons, Loch Ness monsters, mummies...

In fact, you better HOPE it's just a ghost.

Well, how do we find out which one it is?

CHOMP CHOMP

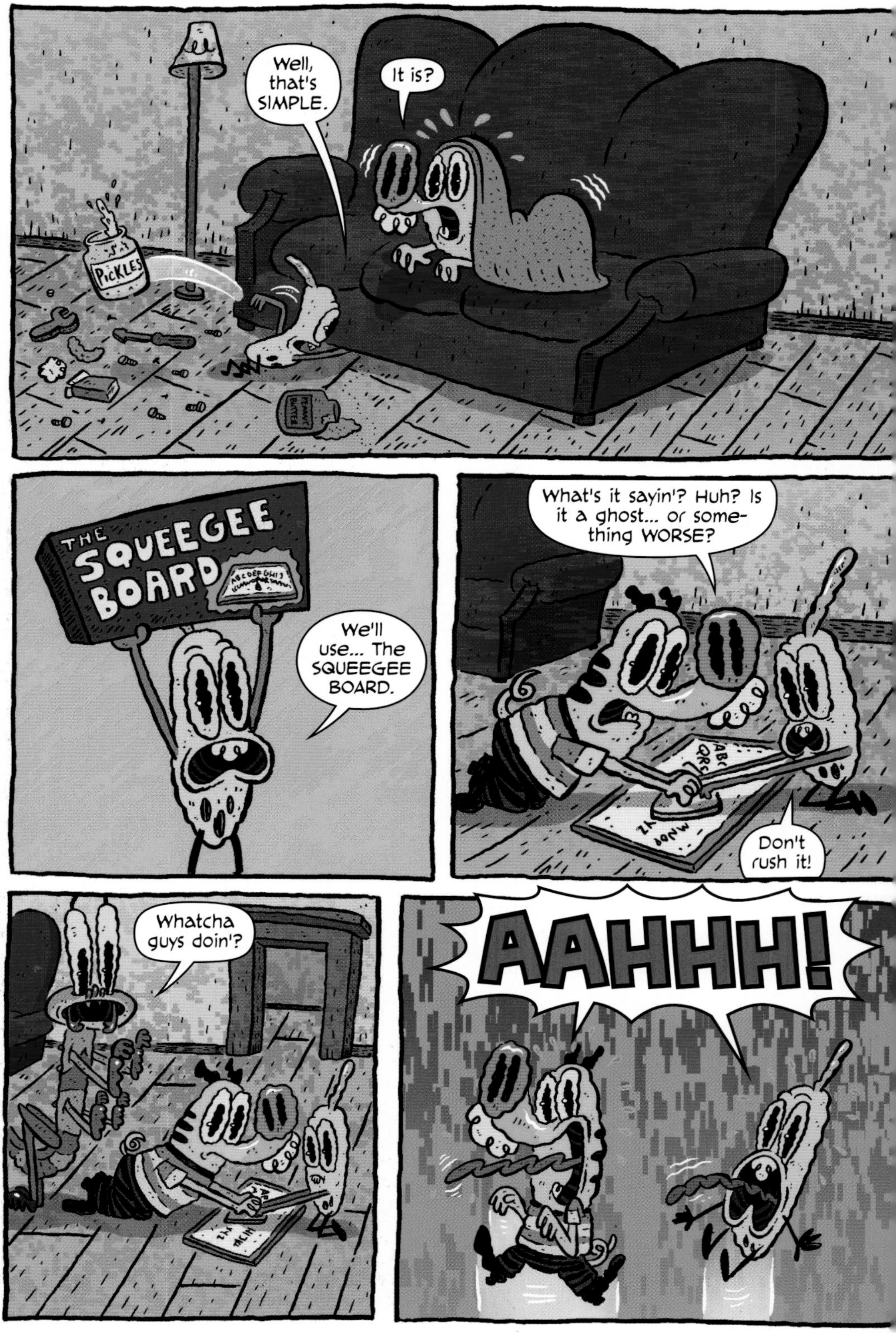
Well, that's SIMPLE.
It is?
PICKLES
PEANUT BUTTER
THE SQUEEGEE BOARD
We'll use... The SQUEEGEE BOARD.
What's it sayin'? Huh? Is it a ghost... or something WORSE?
Don't rush it!
Whatcha guys doin'?
AAHHH!

Oh, it's JUST Cricket!

≥Whew.≤

CRICKET

HA HAHA! Who did you THINK it was, the boogie-man?

We kinda thought you were a... ghost.

A GHOST? Everybody knows that GHOSTS aren't real! HAHAHA!

It's not THAT crazy. It's not like we said we thought you were an ALIEN, or something.

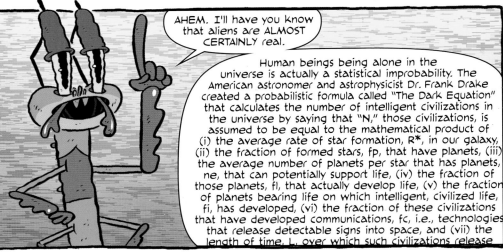

AHEM. I'll have you know that aliens are ALMOST CERTAINLY real.

Human beings being alone in the universe is actually a statistical improbability. The American astronomer and astrophysicist Dr. Frank Drake created a probabilistic formula called "The Dark Equation" that calculates the number of intelligent civilizations in the universe by saying that "N," those civilizations, is assumed to be equal to the mathematical product of (i) the average rate of star formation, R^*, in our galaxy, (ii) the fraction of formed stars, f_p, that have planets, (iii) the average number of planets per star that has planets, n_e, that can potentially support life, (iv) the fraction of those planets, f_l, that actually develop life, (v) the fraction of planets bearing life on which intelligent, civilized life, f_i, has developed, (vi) the fraction of these civilizations that have developed communications, f_c, i.e., technologies that release detectable signs into space, and (vii) the length of time, L, over which such civilizations release

45

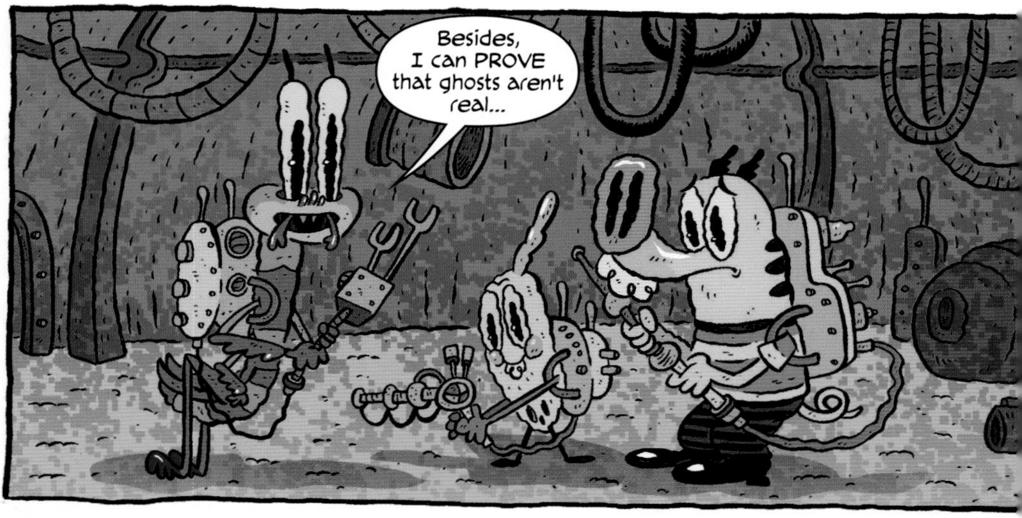
Besides, I can PROVE that ghosts aren't real...

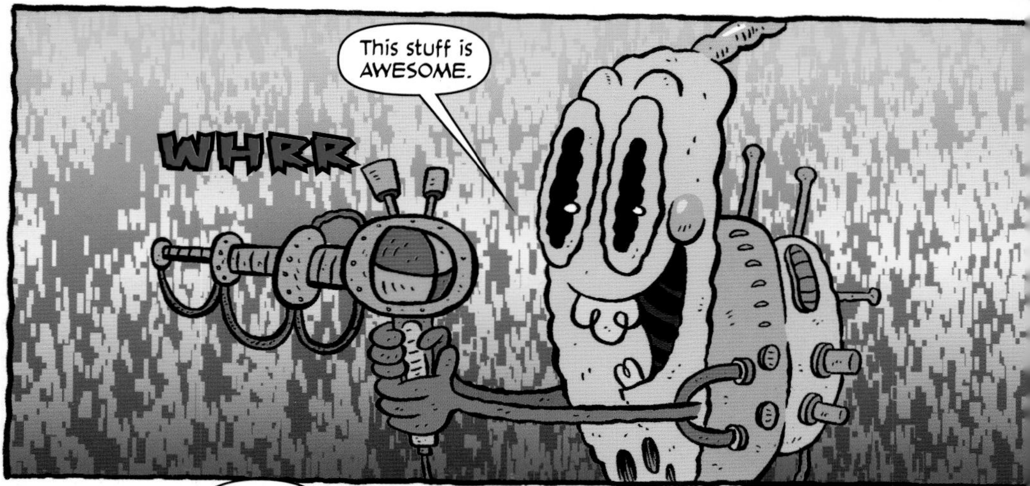
This stuff is AWESOME.
WHRR

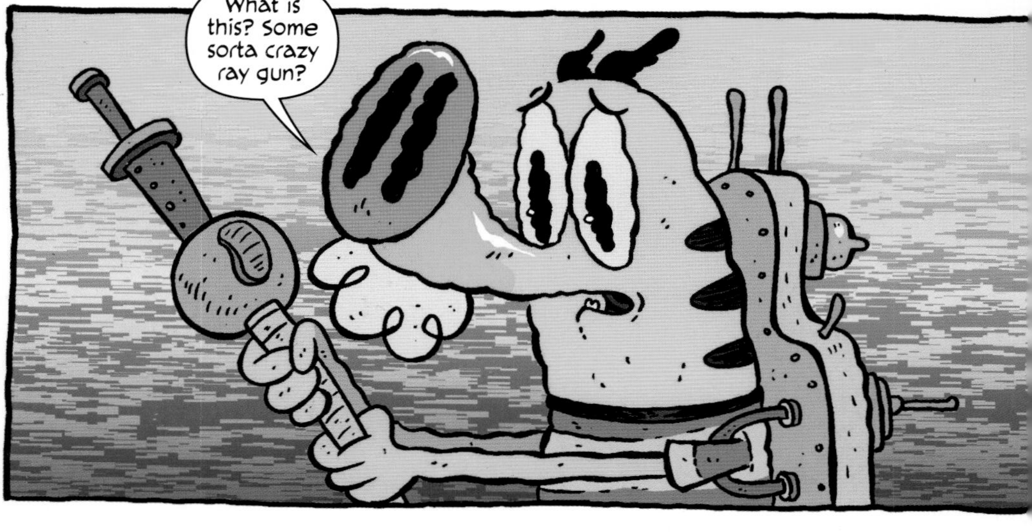
What is this? Some sorta crazy ray gun?

Nothing so crude.

It's actually SUPER SOPHISTICATED spectral tracking equipment.

It detects ghosts?

?

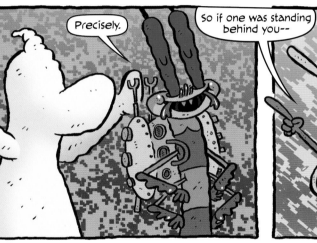

Precisely.

So if one was standing behind you--

Like RIGHT behind you--

--you'd be able to DETECT it?

It's... right behind me, isn't it?

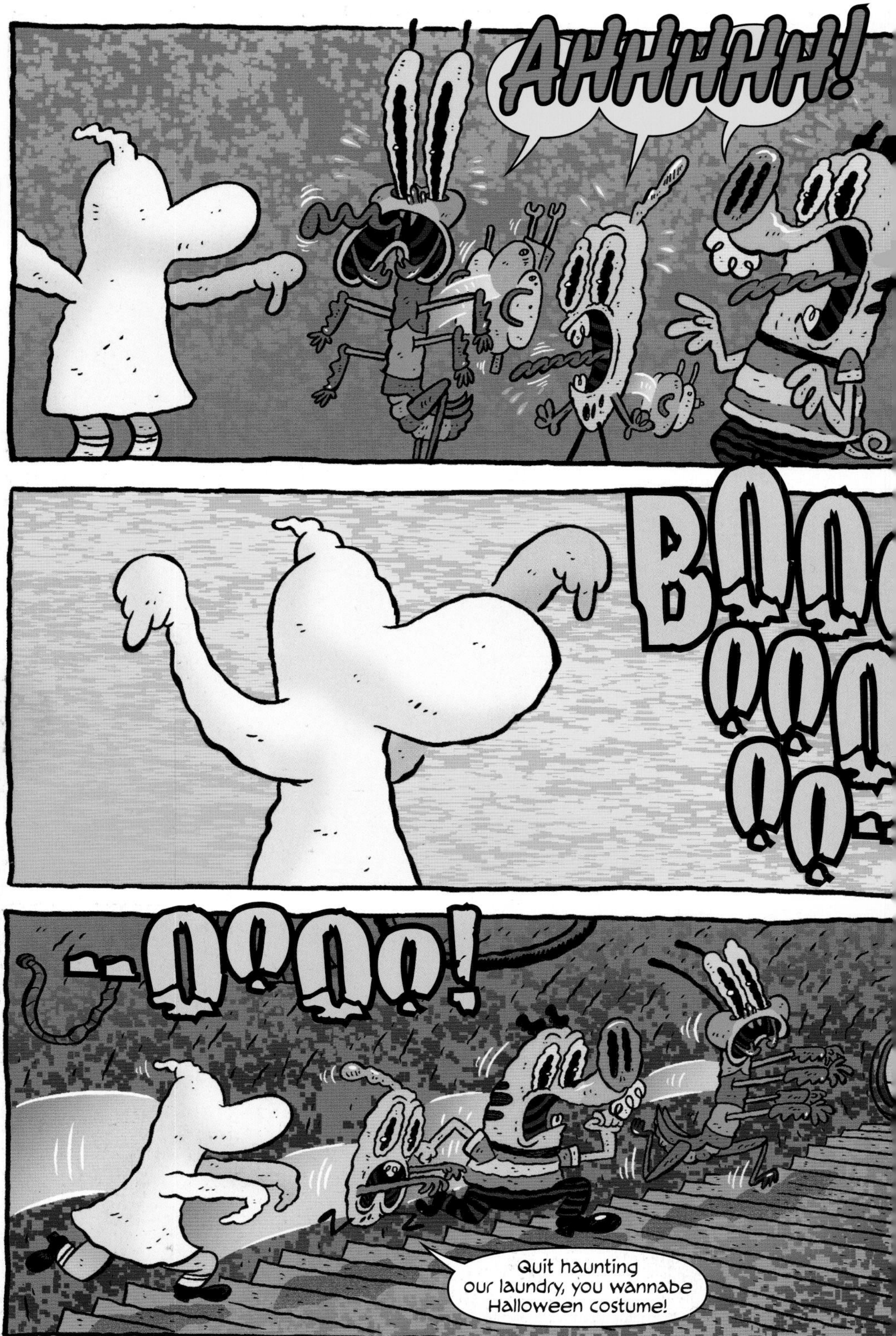
AHHHHHH!
BOOOOOOOOO-
-OOOOO!
Quit haunting our laundry, you wannabe Halloween costume!

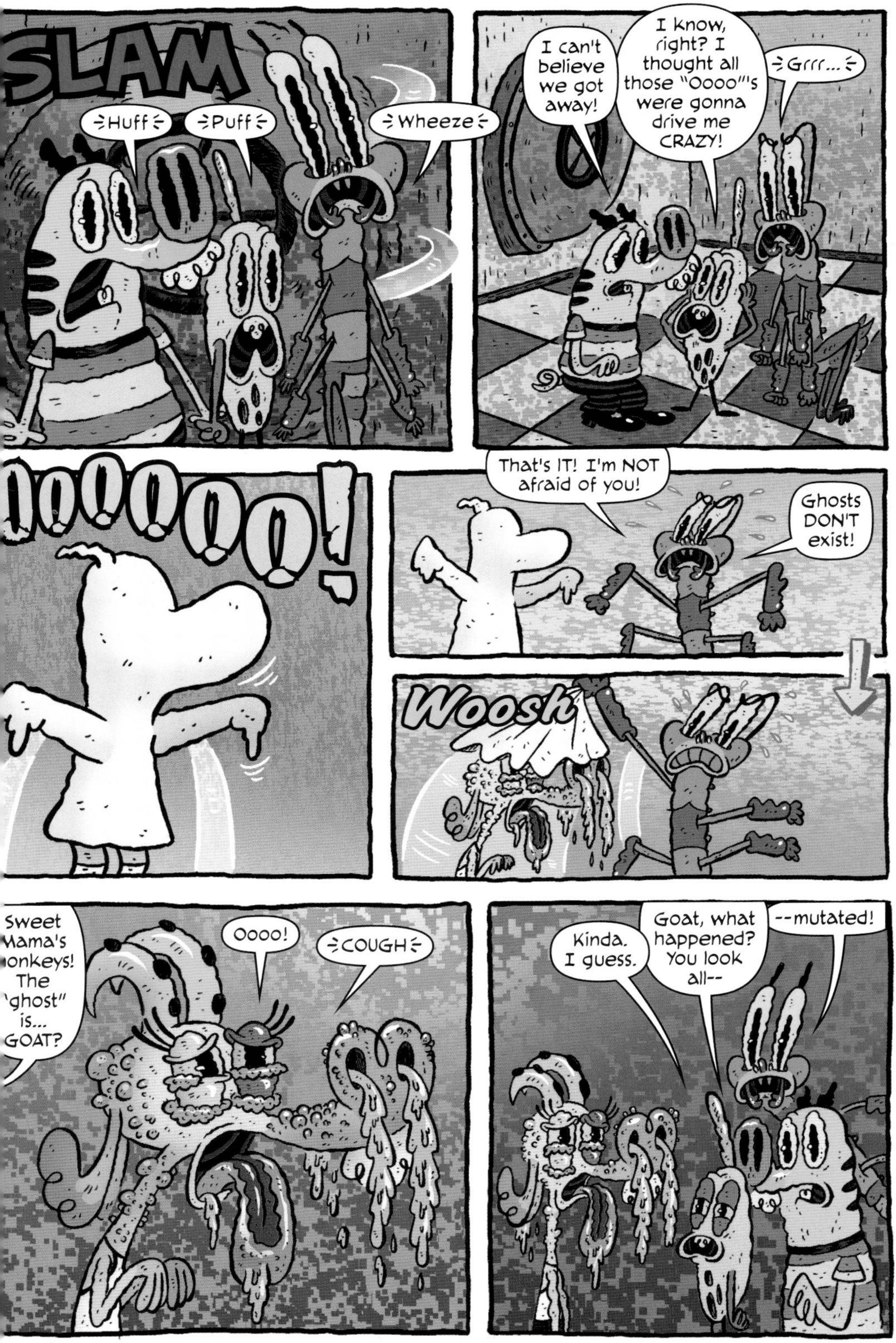
SLAM
Huff
Puff
Wheeze
I can't believe we got away!
I know, right? I thought all those "Oooo"'s were gonna drive me CRAZY!
Grrr...
OOOOOOO!
That's IT! I'm NOT afraid of you!
Ghosts DON'T exist!
Woosh
Sweet Mama's monkeys! The "ghost" is... GOAT?
Oooo!
COUGH
Kinda. I guess.
Goat, what happened? You look all--
--mutated!

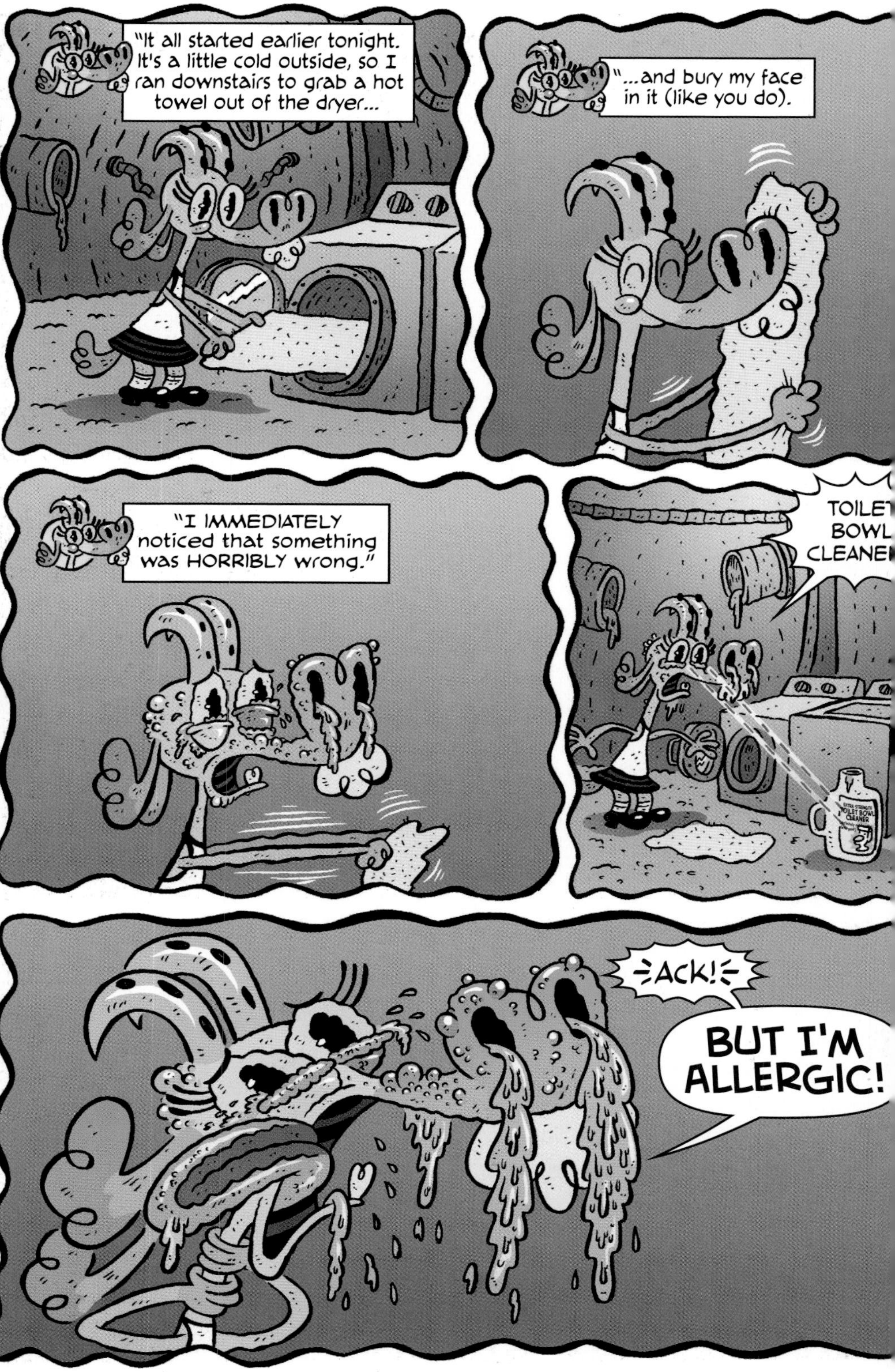
"It all started earlier tonight. It's a little cold outside, so I ran downstairs to grab a hot towel out of the dryer...
"...and bury my face in it (like you do).
"I IMMEDIATELY noticed that something was HORRIBLY wrong."
TOILET BOWL CLEANE
ACK!
BUT I'M ALLERGIC!

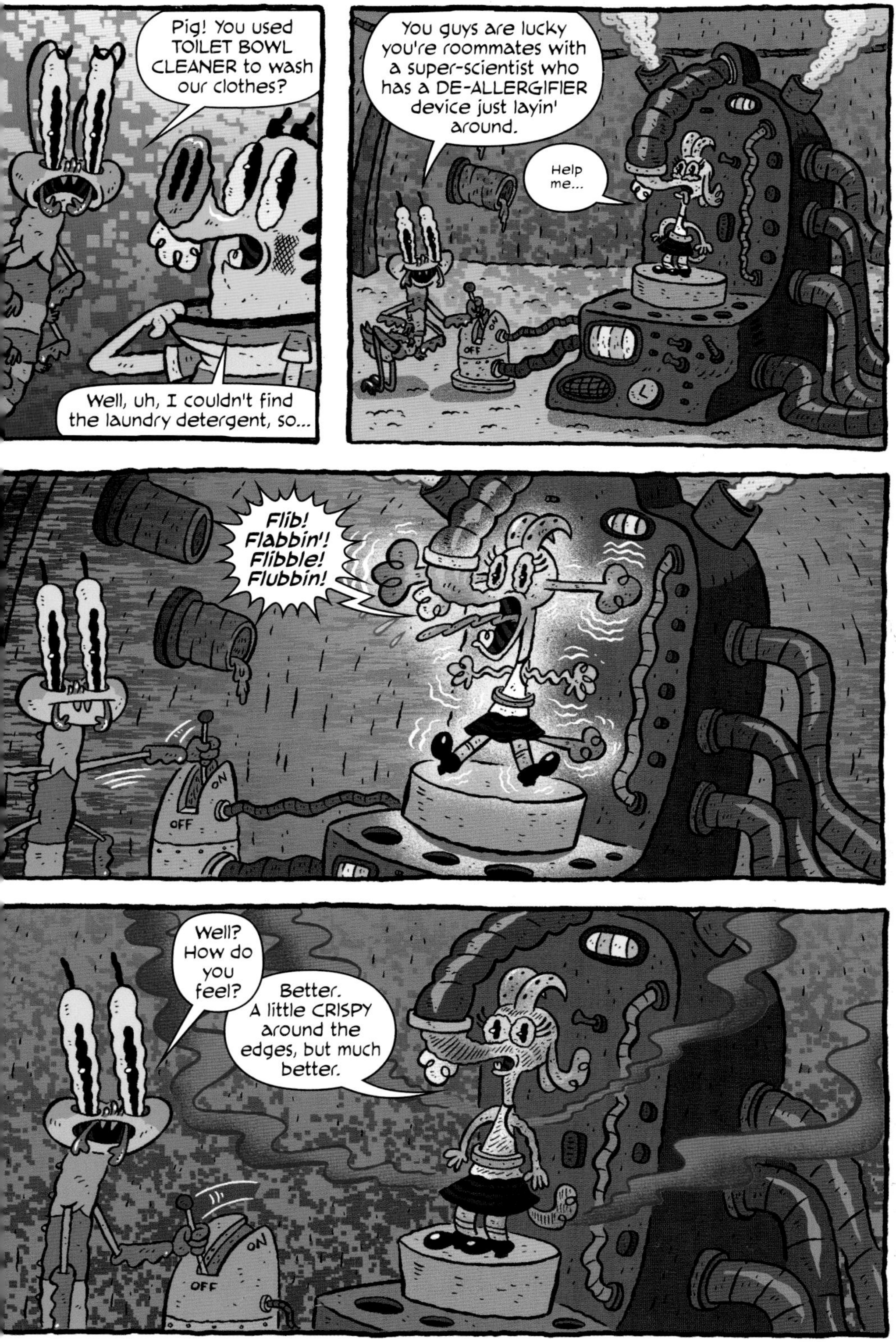
Pig! You used TOILET BOWL CLEANER to wash our clothes?
Well, uh, I couldn't find the laundry detergent, so...
You guys are lucky you're roommates with a super-scientist who has a DE-ALLERGIFIER device just layin' around.
Help me...
ON
OFF
Flib! Flabbin'! Flibble! Flubbin!
ON
OFF
Well? How do you feel?
Better. A little CRISPY around the edges, but much better.
ON
OFF

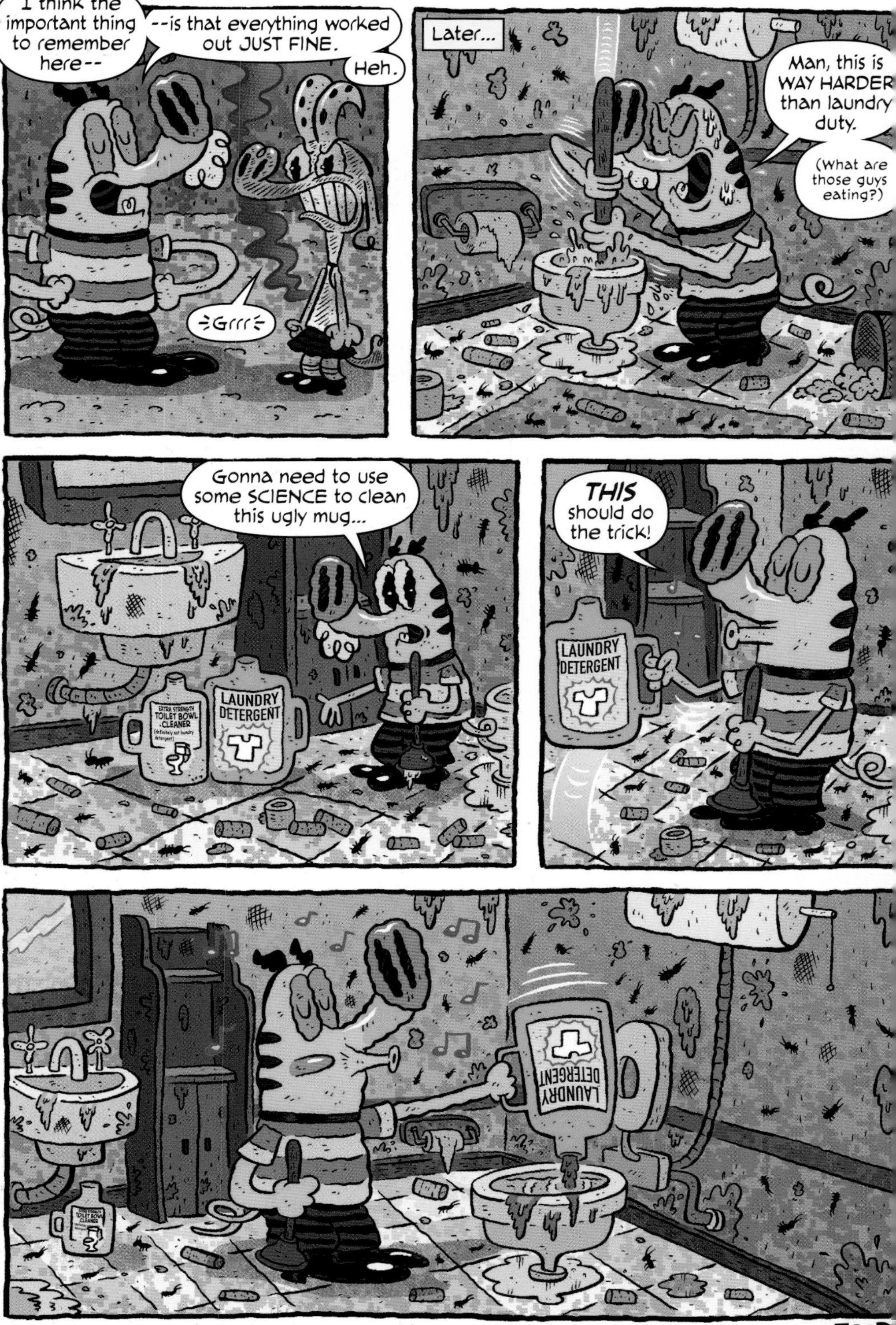
I think the important thing to remember here--
--is that everything worked out JUST FINE.
Heh.
Grrr
Later...
Man, this is WAY HARDER than laundry duty.
(What are those guys eating?)
Gonna need to use some SCIENCE to clean this ugly mug...
EXTRA STRENGTH TOILET BOWL CLEANER
LAUNDRY DETERGENT
THIS should do the trick!
LAUNDRY DETERGENT
LAUNDRY DETERGENT
END

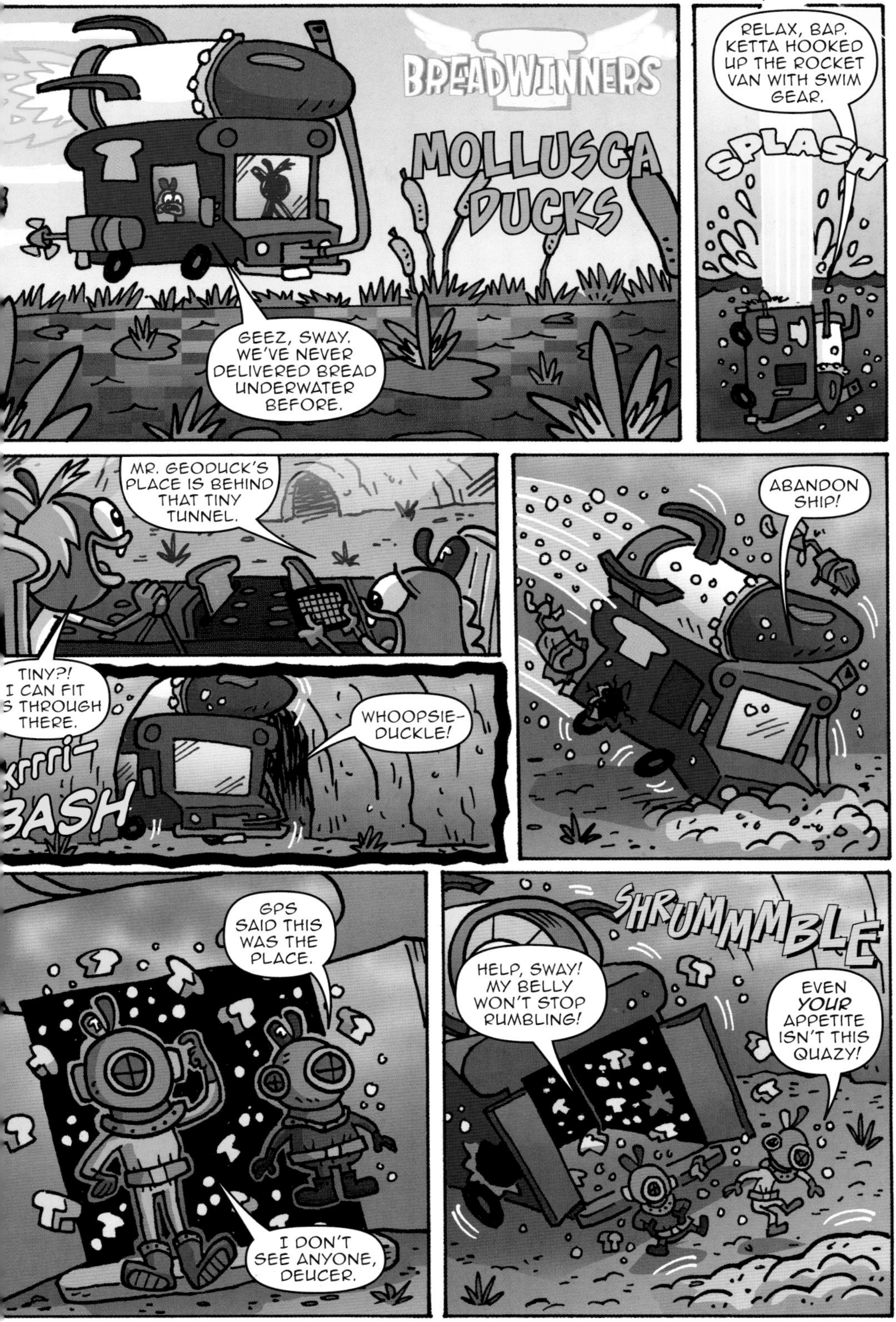
BREADWINNERS
MOLLUSCA DUCKS
GEEZ, SWAY. WE'VE NEVER DELIVERED BREAD UNDERWATER BEFORE.
RELAX, BAP. KETTA HOOKED UP THE ROCKET VAN WITH SWIM GEAR.
SPLASH
MR. GEODUCK'S PLACE IS BEHIND THAT TINY TUNNEL.
TINY?! I CAN FIT S THROUGH THERE.
krrri-
BASH
WHOOPSIE-DUCKLE!
ABANDON SHIP!
GPS SAID THIS WAS THE PLACE.
I DON'T SEE ANYONE, DEUCER.
SHRUMMMBLE
HELP, SWAY! MY BELLY WON'T STOP RUMBLING!
EVEN YOUR APPETITE ISN'T THIS QUAZY!

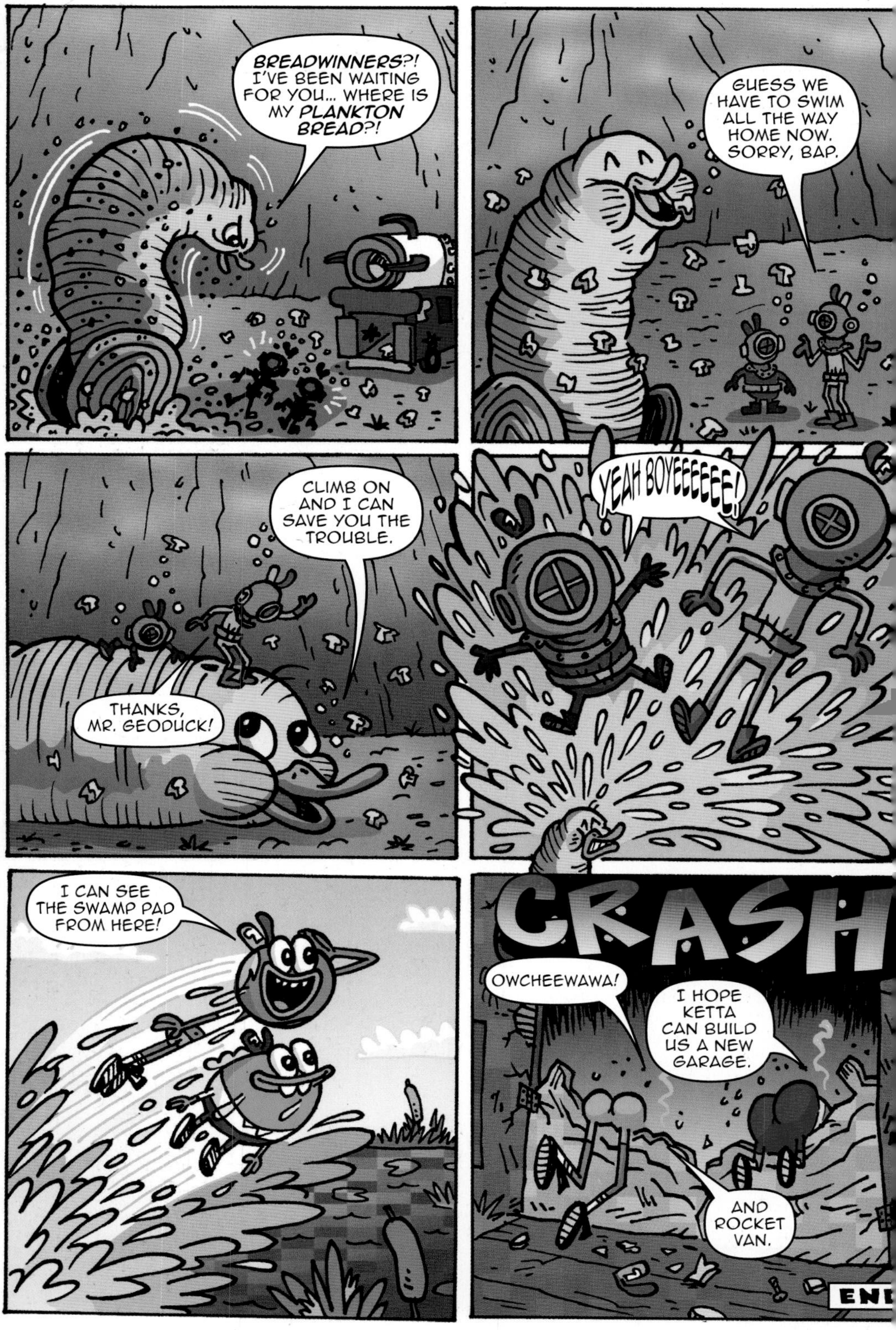
BREADWINNERS?! I'VE BEEN WAITING FOR YOU... WHERE IS MY PLANKTON BREAD?!
GUESS WE HAVE TO SWIM ALL THE WAY HOME NOW. SORRY, BAP.
CLIMB ON AND I CAN SAVE YOU THE TROUBLE.
THANKS, MR. GEODUCK!
YEAH BOYEEEEEE!
I CAN SEE THE SWAMP PAD FROM HERE!
CRASH
OWCHEEWAWA!
I HOPE KETTA CAN BUILD US A NEW GARAGE.
AND ROCKET VAN.

DID YOU KNOW SOME PIRATES AREN'T VERY GOOD AT HIDING THEIR BOOTY?

SHUT UP, FOO! CAPTAIN NO-BEARD IS COMING!

THIS PIRATE AIN'T GOT AN EYE-PATCH OR A HOOKY-HAND, BUT HE DOES HAVE LOTS OF TREASURE!

AND EVERY DAY, HE GOES AROUND HIDING IT IN LIL' TREASURE CHESTS! RIGHT THERE IN THE OPEN LIKE A BIG DUMMY!

THEN, AFTER HE LEAVES TO GO DO PIRATE STUFF, ME AND FEE PLUNDER HIS LOOT!-- P.S. I DON'T KNOW WHAT PLUNDER OR LOOT MEANS!

YOU FIND ANY COOL PIRATE STUFF TODAY, SIS?

NAH, JUST A BUNCHA WORDY PAPERS...

COLLEGE ACCEPTANCE LETTER

EVEN THOUGH THERE'S NEVER ANY GOLD OR WOODEN LEGS, PIRATE BOOTY IS STILL AAAAAAARESOME!

EXTRA-STRENGTH DEODORANT

OOO! I FOUND PIRATE CANDY!

MMM! TASTES LIKE A MINTY FINGERNAIL!

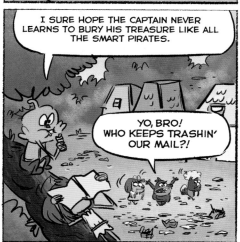

I SURE HOPE THE CAPTAIN NEVER LEARNS TO BURY HIS TREASURE LIKE ALL THE SMART PIRATES.

YO, BRO! WHO KEEPS TRASHIN' OUR MAIL?!

GUYS, JUST A HEADS UP, IF YOU SMELL ANYTHING TERRIBLE AND NOT MINTY, IT'S DEFINITELY ME.

SCHUSTER

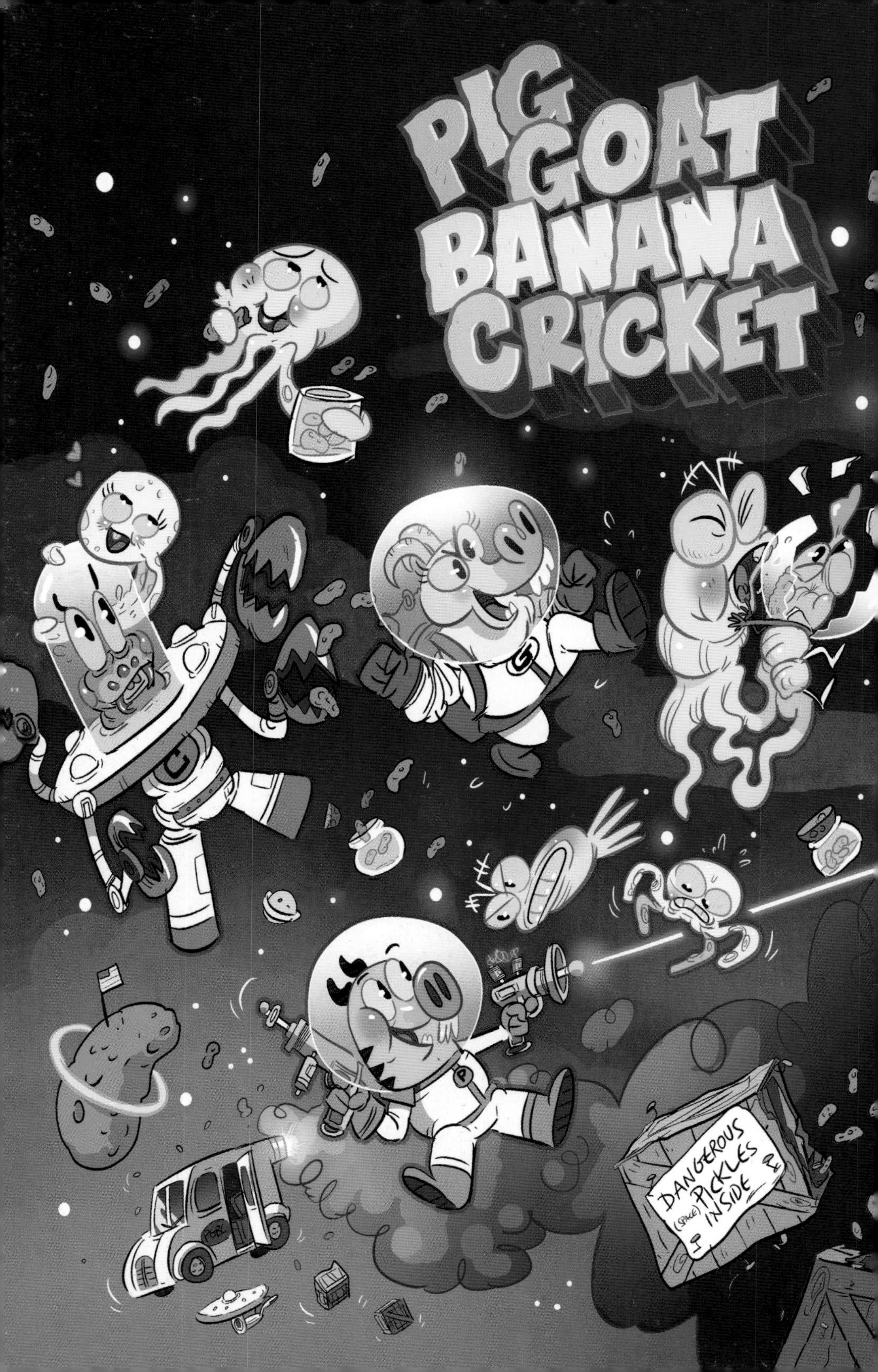
PIG GOAT BANANA CRICKET
DANGEROUS (SPACE) PICKLES INSIDE

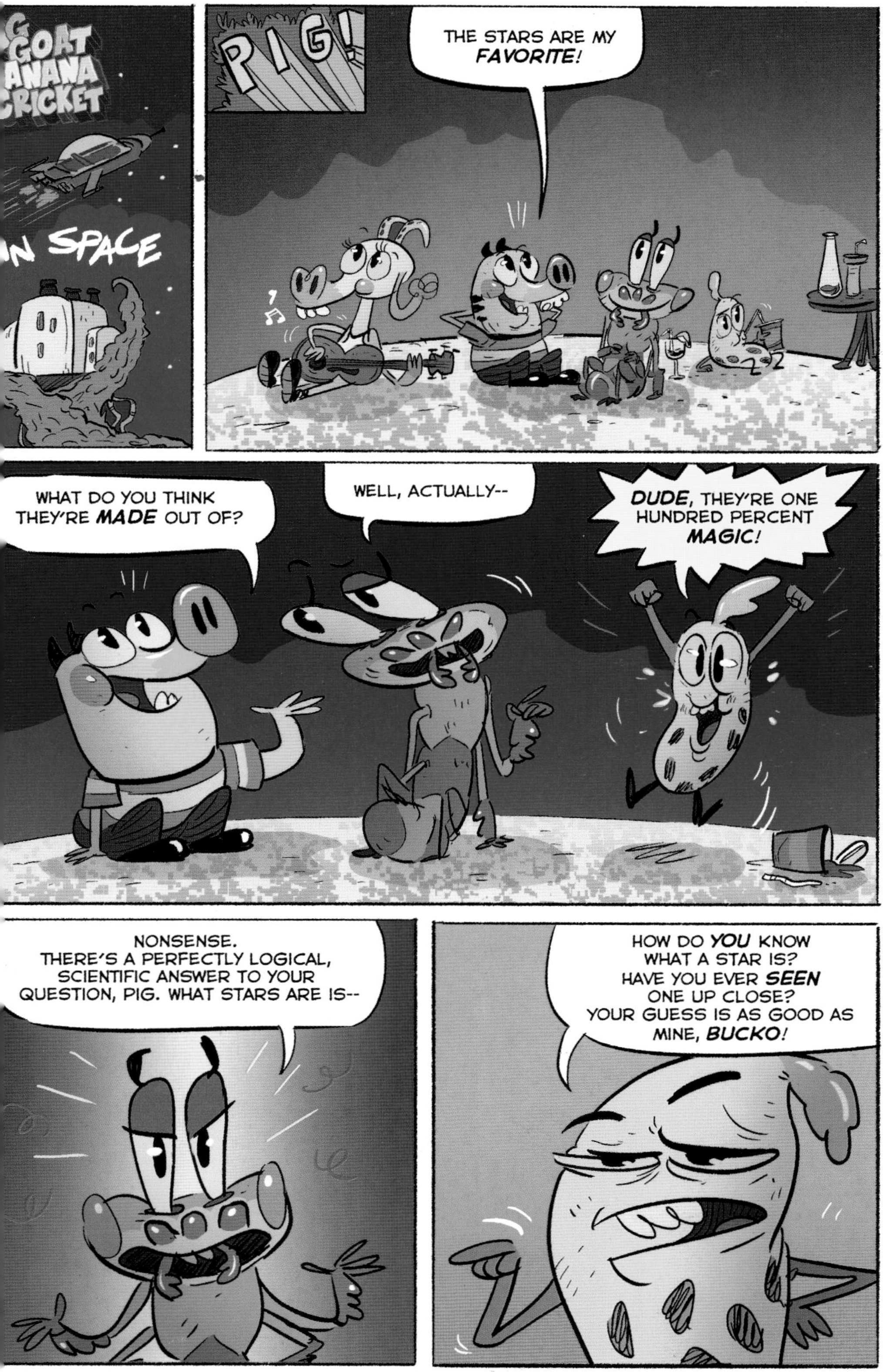
G GOAT
ANANA
CRICKET
N SPACE
PIG!
THE STARS ARE MY *FAVORITE!*
WHAT DO YOU THINK THEY'RE *MADE* OUT OF?
WELL, ACTUALLY--
DUDE, THEY'RE ONE HUNDRED PERCENT *MAGIC!*
NONSENSE. THERE'S A PERFECTLY LOGICAL, SCIENTIFIC ANSWER TO YOUR QUESTION, PIG. WHAT STARS ARE IS--
HOW DO *YOU* KNOW WHAT A STAR IS? HAVE YOU EVER *SEEN* ONE UP CLOSE? YOUR GUESS IS AS GOOD AS MINE, *BUCKO!*

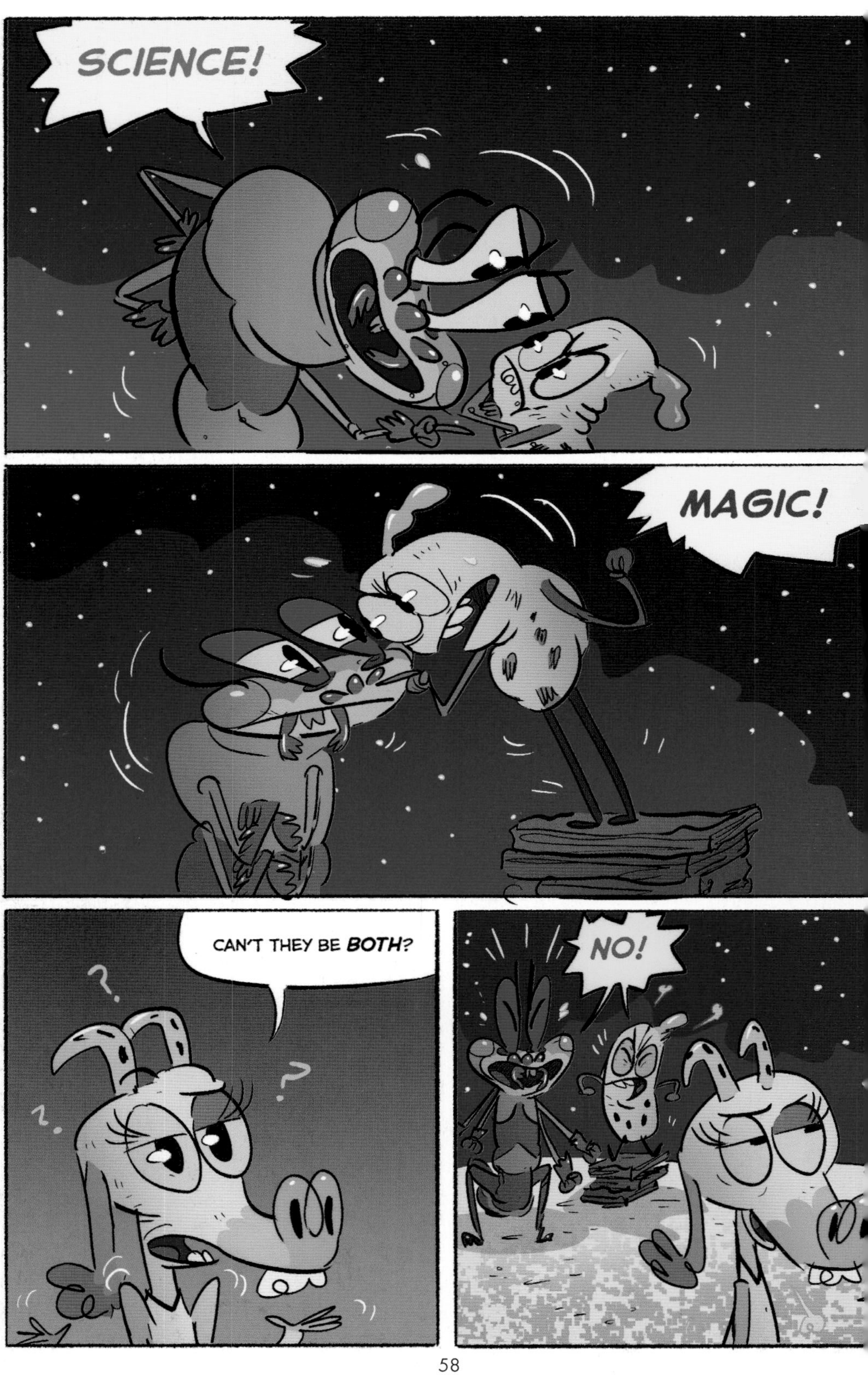
SCIENCE!
MAGIC!
CAN'T THEY BE BOTH?
NO!

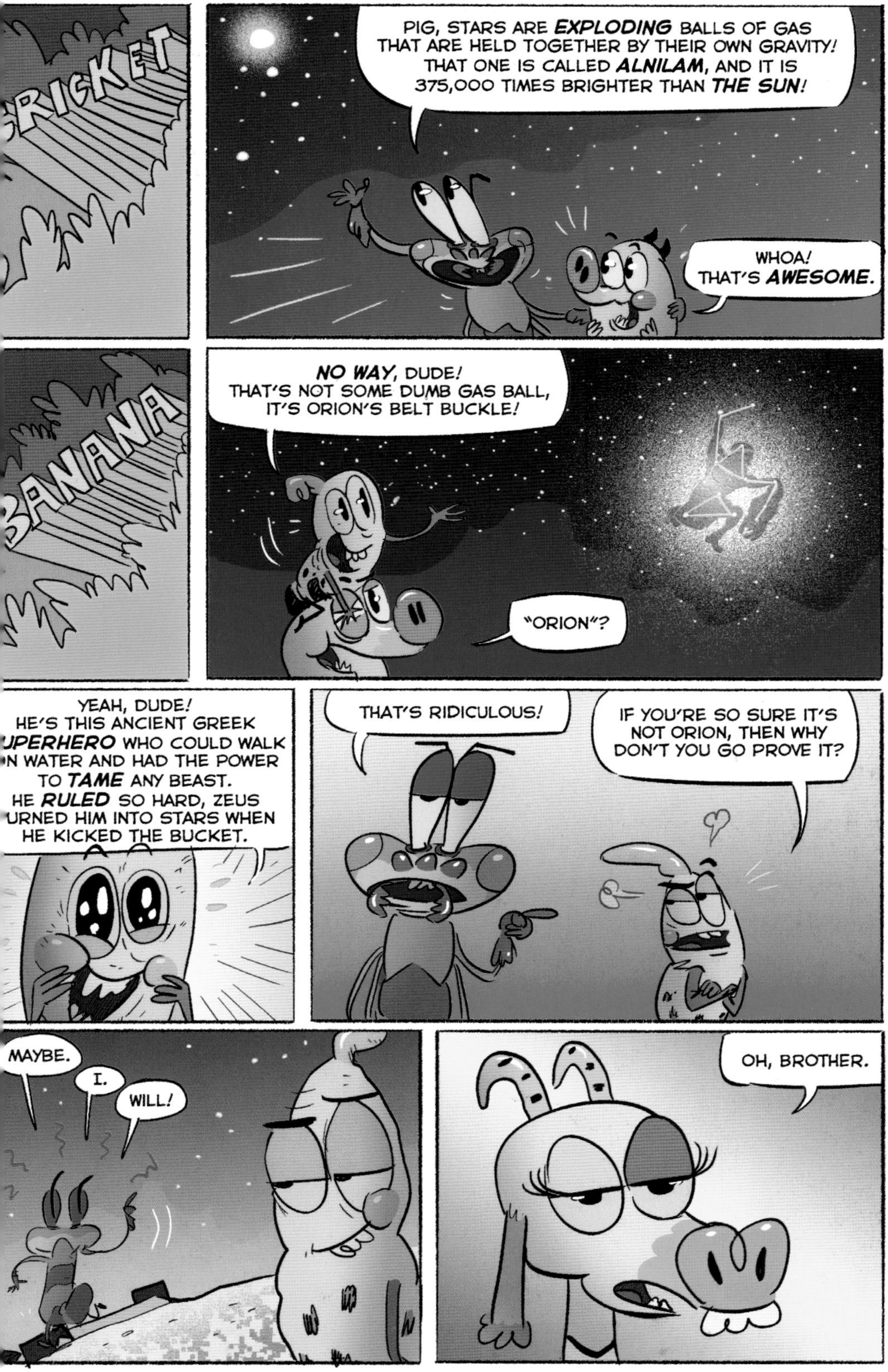
CRICKET
PIG, STARS ARE EXPLODING BALLS OF GAS THAT ARE HELD TOGETHER BY THEIR OWN GRAVITY! THAT ONE IS CALLED ALNILAM, AND IT IS 375,000 TIMES BRIGHTER THAN THE SUN!
WHOA! THAT'S AWESOME.
BANANA
NO WAY, DUDE! THAT'S NOT SOME DUMB GAS BALL, IT'S ORION'S BELT BUCKLE!
"ORION"?
YEAH, DUDE! HE'S THIS ANCIENT GREEK UPERHERO WHO COULD WALK N WATER AND HAD THE POWER TO TAME ANY BEAST. HE RULED SO HARD, ZEUS URNED HIM INTO STARS WHEN HE KICKED THE BUCKET.
THAT'S RIDICULOUS!
IF YOU'RE SO SURE IT'S NOT ORION, THEN WHY DON'T YOU GO PROVE IT?
MAYBE.
I.
WILL!
OH, BROTHER.

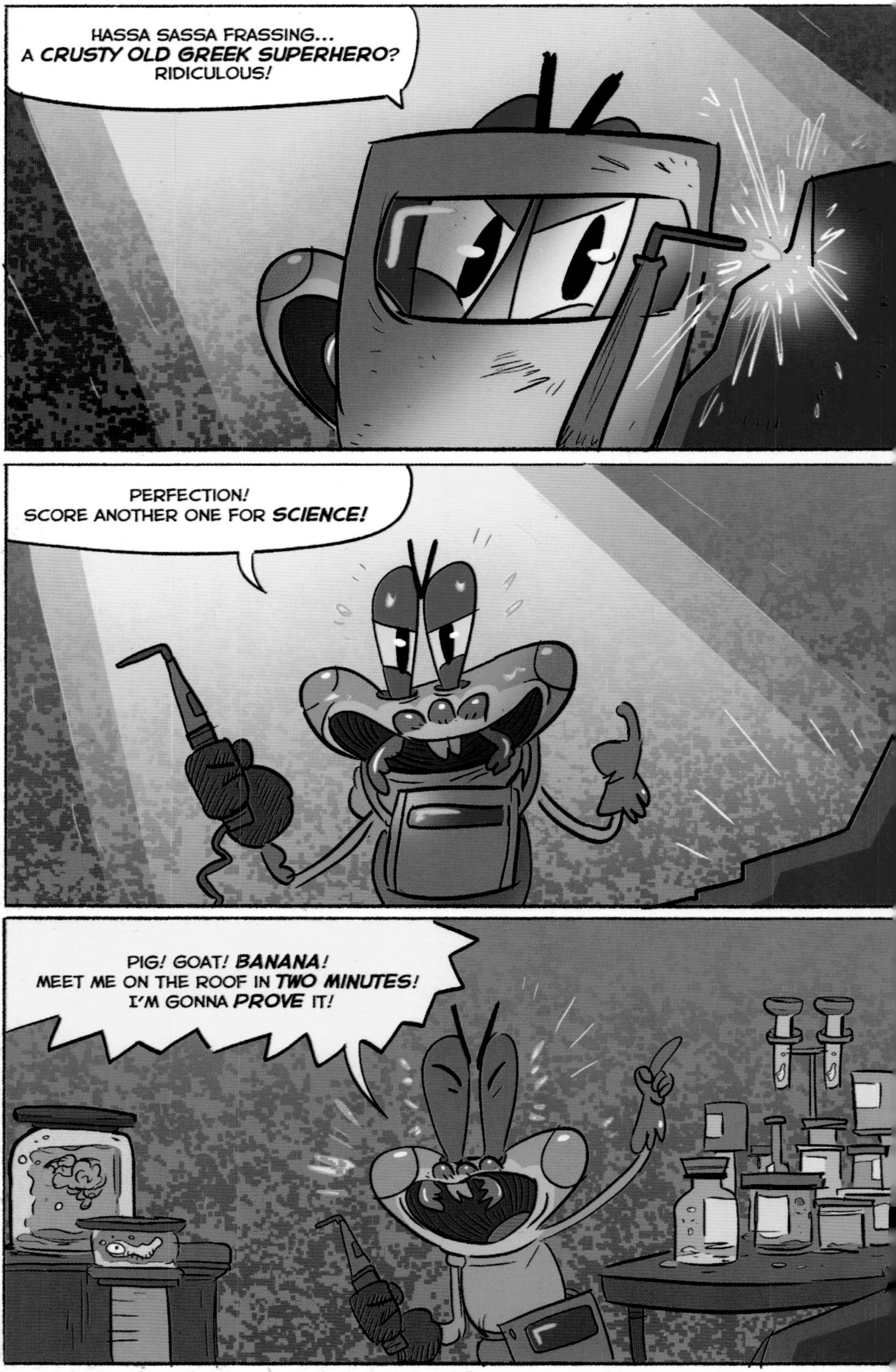
HASSA SASSA FRASSING...
A *CRUSTY OLD GREEK SUPERHERO*? RIDICULOUS!
PERFECTION! SCORE ANOTHER ONE FOR *SCIENCE!*
PIG! GOAT! *BANANA!* MEET ME ON THE ROOF IN *TWO MINUTES!* I'M GONNA *PROVE* IT!

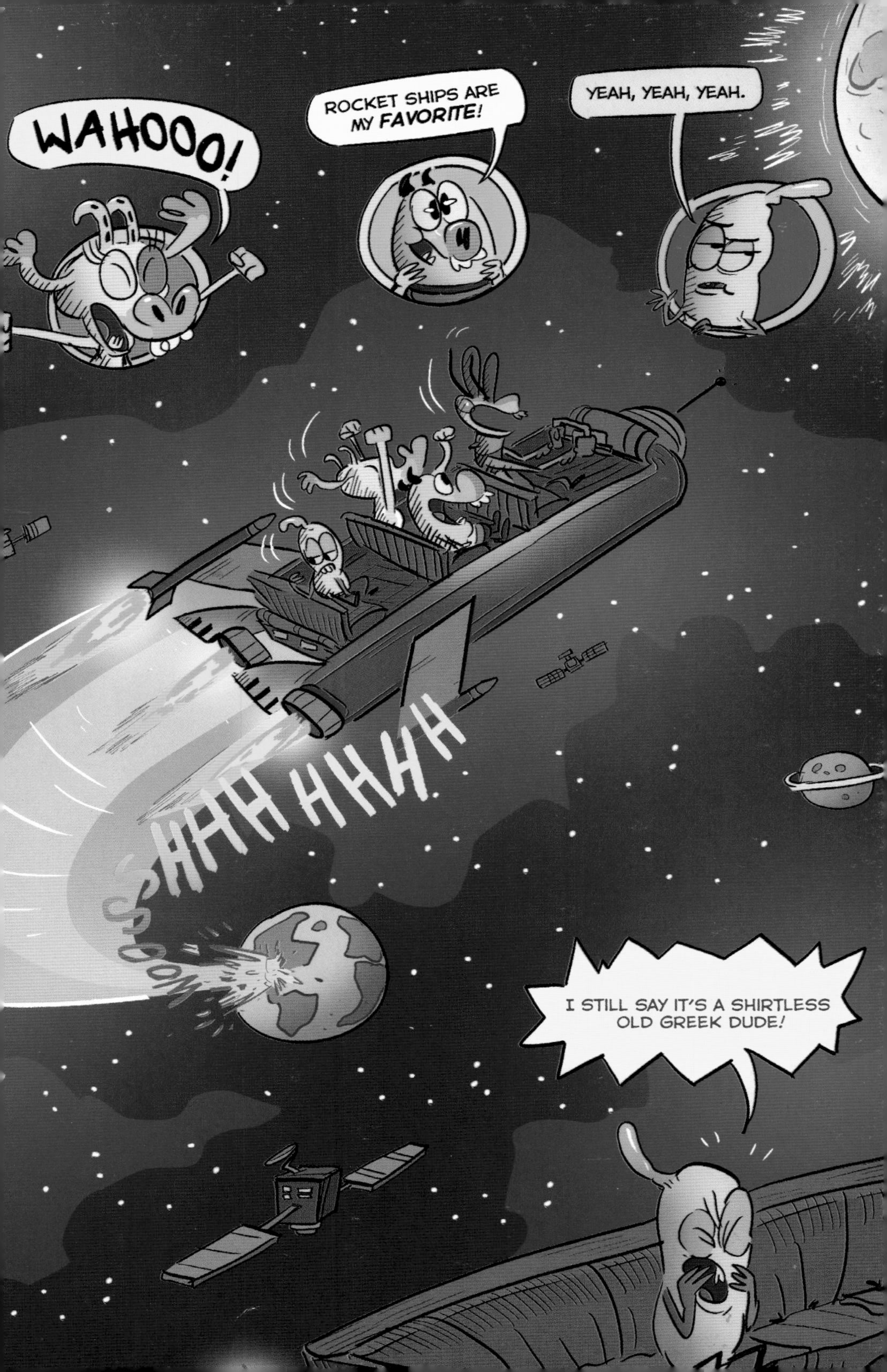
WAHOOO!
ROCKET SHIPS ARE MY *FAVORITE!*
YEAH, YEAH, YEAH.
SHHHHHHH
SPOOOSH
I STILL SAY IT'S A SHIRTLESS OLD GREEK DUDE!

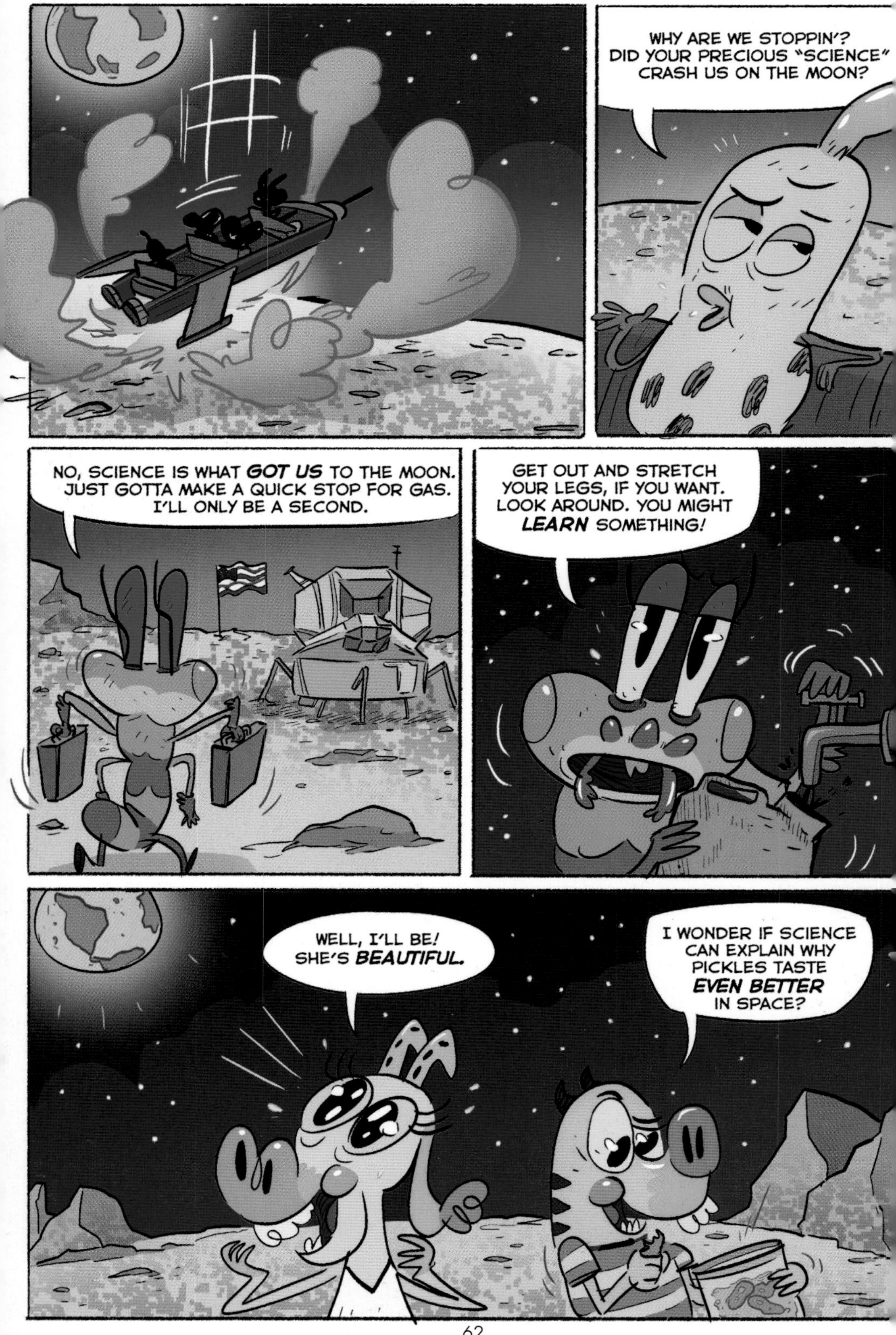
WHY ARE WE STOPPIN'? DID YOUR PRECIOUS "SCIENCE" CRASH US ON THE MOON?
NO, SCIENCE IS WHAT **GOT US** TO THE MOON. JUST GOTTA MAKE A QUICK STOP FOR GAS. I'LL ONLY BE A SECOND.
GET OUT AND STRETCH YOUR LEGS, IF YOU WANT. LOOK AROUND. YOU MIGHT **LEARN** SOMETHING!
WELL, I'LL BE! SHE'S **BEAUTIFUL.**
I WONDER IF SCIENCE CAN EXPLAIN WHY PICKLES TASTE **EVEN BETTER** IN SPACE?

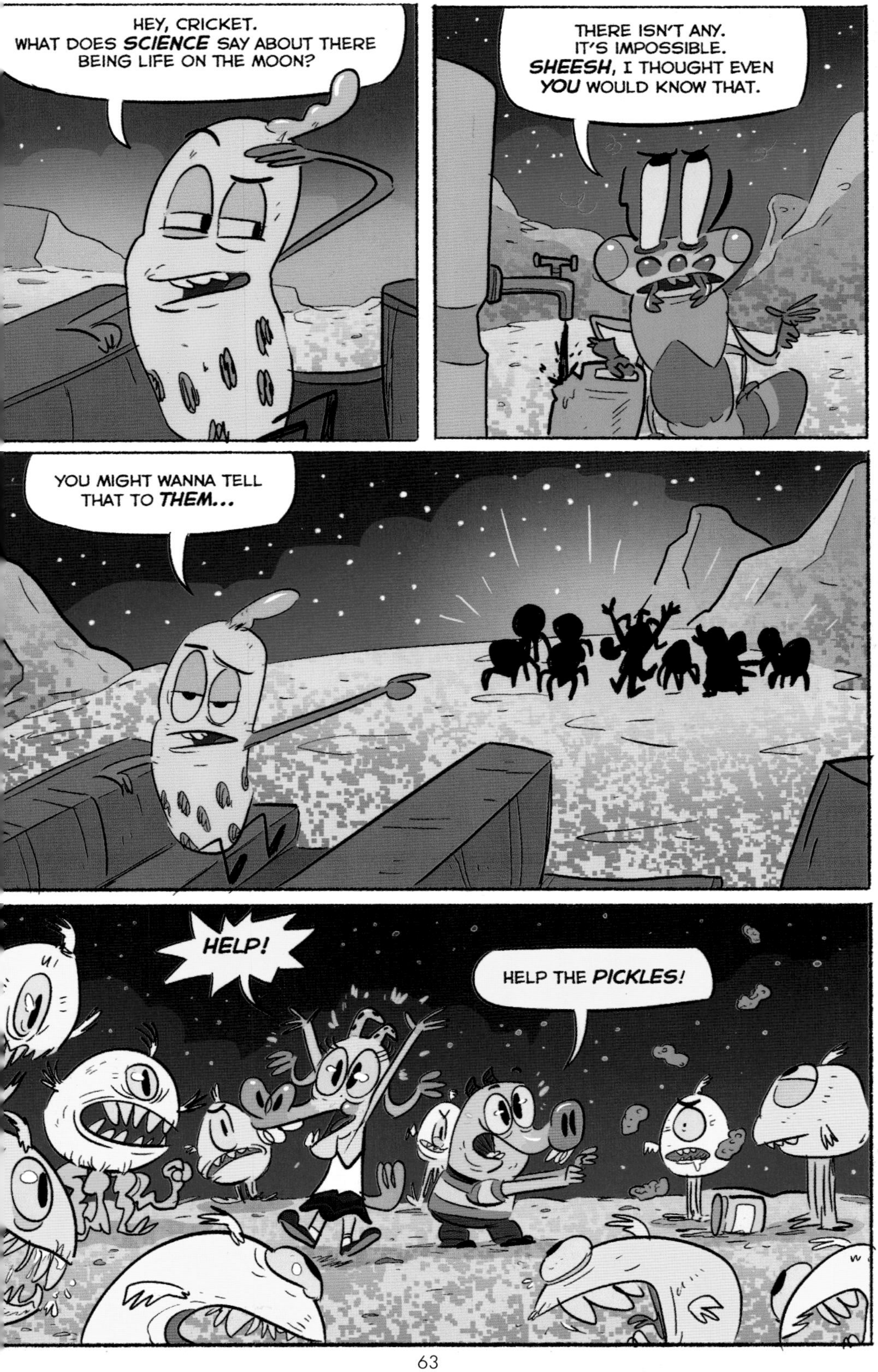
HEY, CRICKET. WHAT DOES SCIENCE SAY ABOUT THERE BEING LIFE ON THE MOON?
THERE ISN'T ANY. IT'S IMPOSSIBLE. SHEESH, I THOUGHT EVEN YOU WOULD KNOW THAT.
YOU MIGHT WANNA TELL THAT TO THEM...
HELP!
HELP THE PICKLES!

BUT THAT'S *IMPOSSIBLE!*

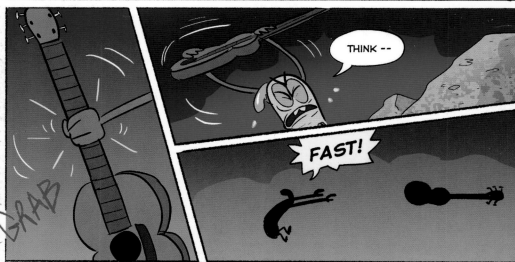

THINK --

FAST!

GRAB

I'M *TRYING!*

NOT *YOU,* GREEN JEANS!
HER!

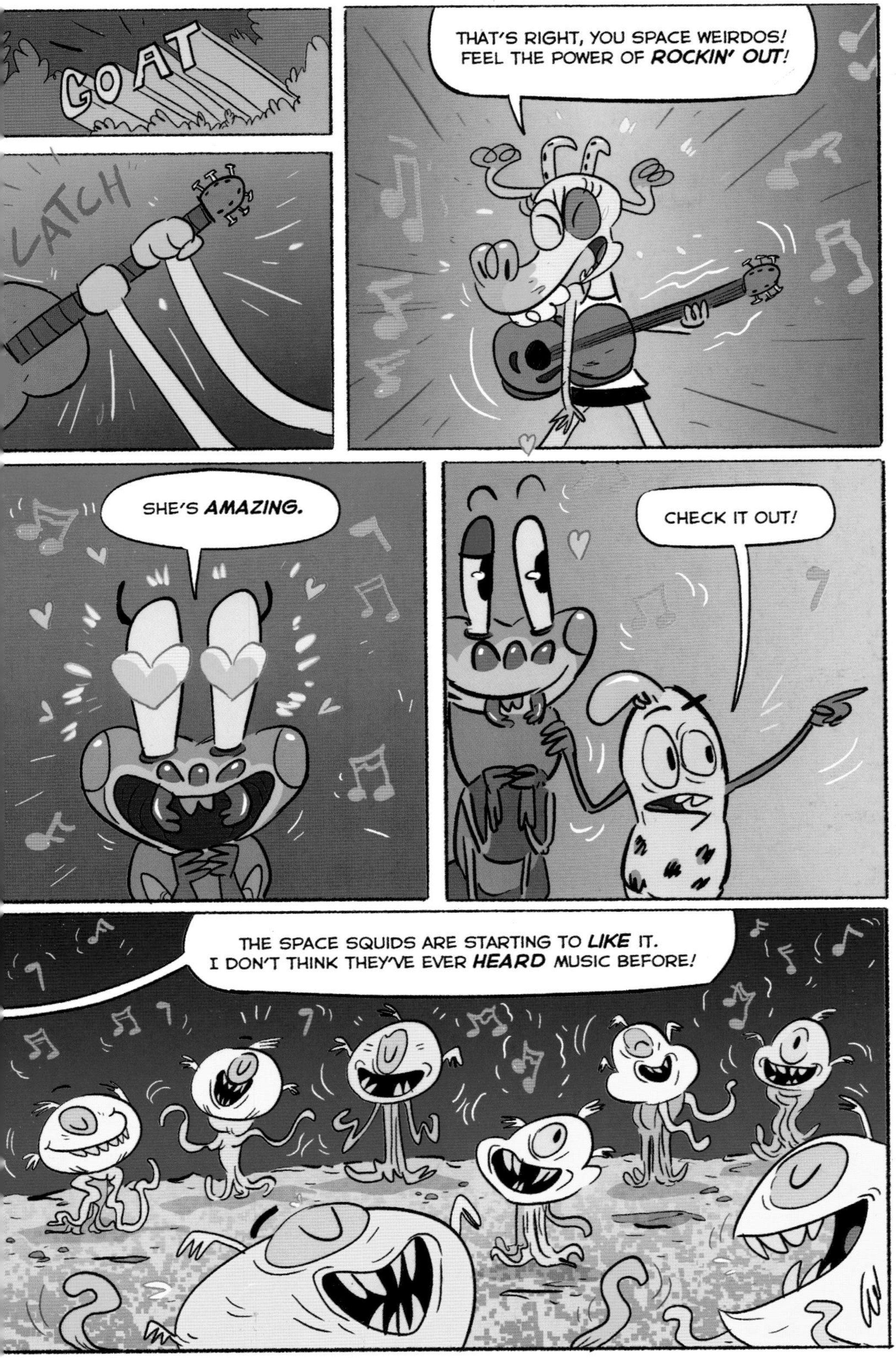
GOAT
CATCH
THAT'S RIGHT, YOU SPACE WEIRDOS! FEEL THE POWER OF ROCKIN' OUT!
SHE'S AMAZING.
CHECK IT OUT!
THE SPACE SQUIDS ARE STARTING TO LIKE IT. I DON'T THINK THEY'VE EVER HEARD MUSIC BEFORE!

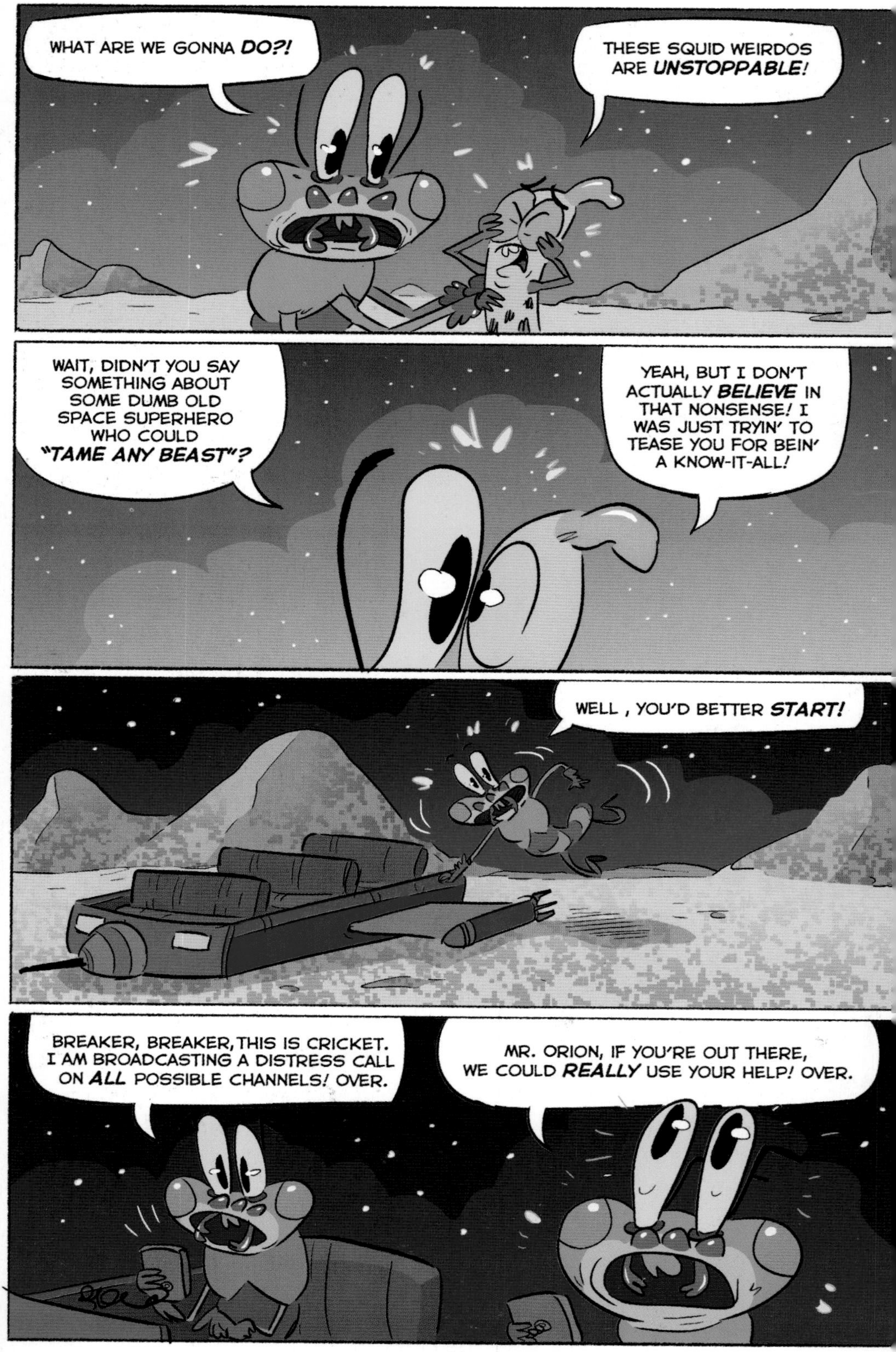
WHAT ARE WE GONNA *DO?!*
THESE SQUID WEIRDOS ARE ***UNSTOPPABLE!***
WAIT, DIDN'T YOU SAY SOMETHING ABOUT SOME DUMB OLD SPACE SUPERHERO WHO COULD ***"TAME ANY BEAST"?***
YEAH, BUT I DON'T ACTUALLY ***BELIEVE*** IN THAT NONSENSE! I WAS JUST TRYIN' TO TEASE YOU FOR BEIN' A KNOW-IT-ALL!
WELL , YOU'D BETTER ***START!***
BREAKER, BREAKER, THIS IS CRICKET. I AM BROADCASTING A DISTRESS CALL ON ***ALL*** POSSIBLE CHANNELS! OVER.
MR. ORION, IF YOU'RE OUT THERE, WE COULD ***REALLY*** USE YOUR HELP! OVER.

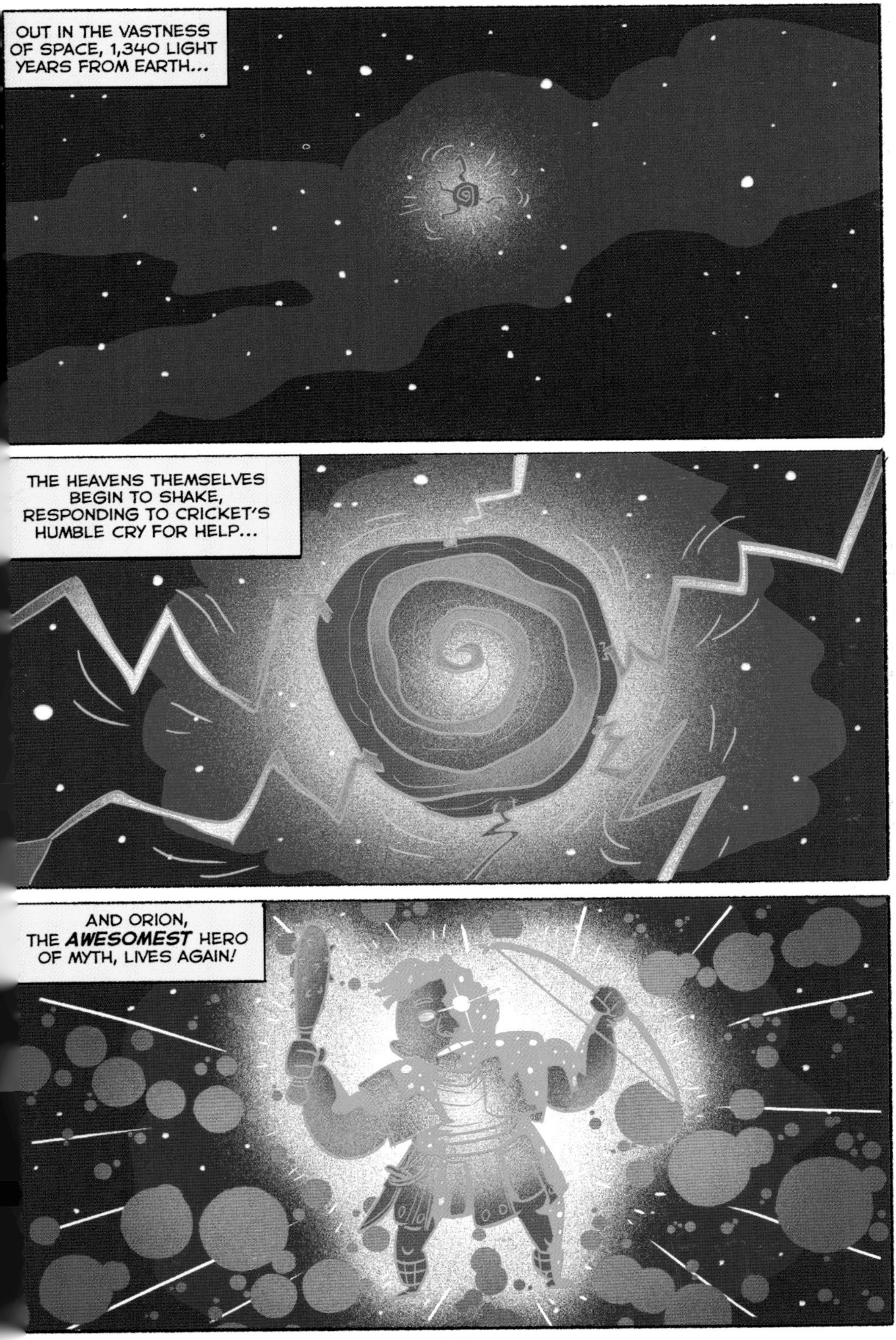
OUT IN THE VASTNESS OF SPACE, 1,340 LIGHT YEARS FROM EARTH...
THE HEAVENS THEMSELVES BEGIN TO SHAKE, RESPONDING TO CRICKET'S HUMBLE CRY FOR HELP...
AND ORION, THE *AWESOMEST* HERO OF MYTH, LIVES AGAIN!

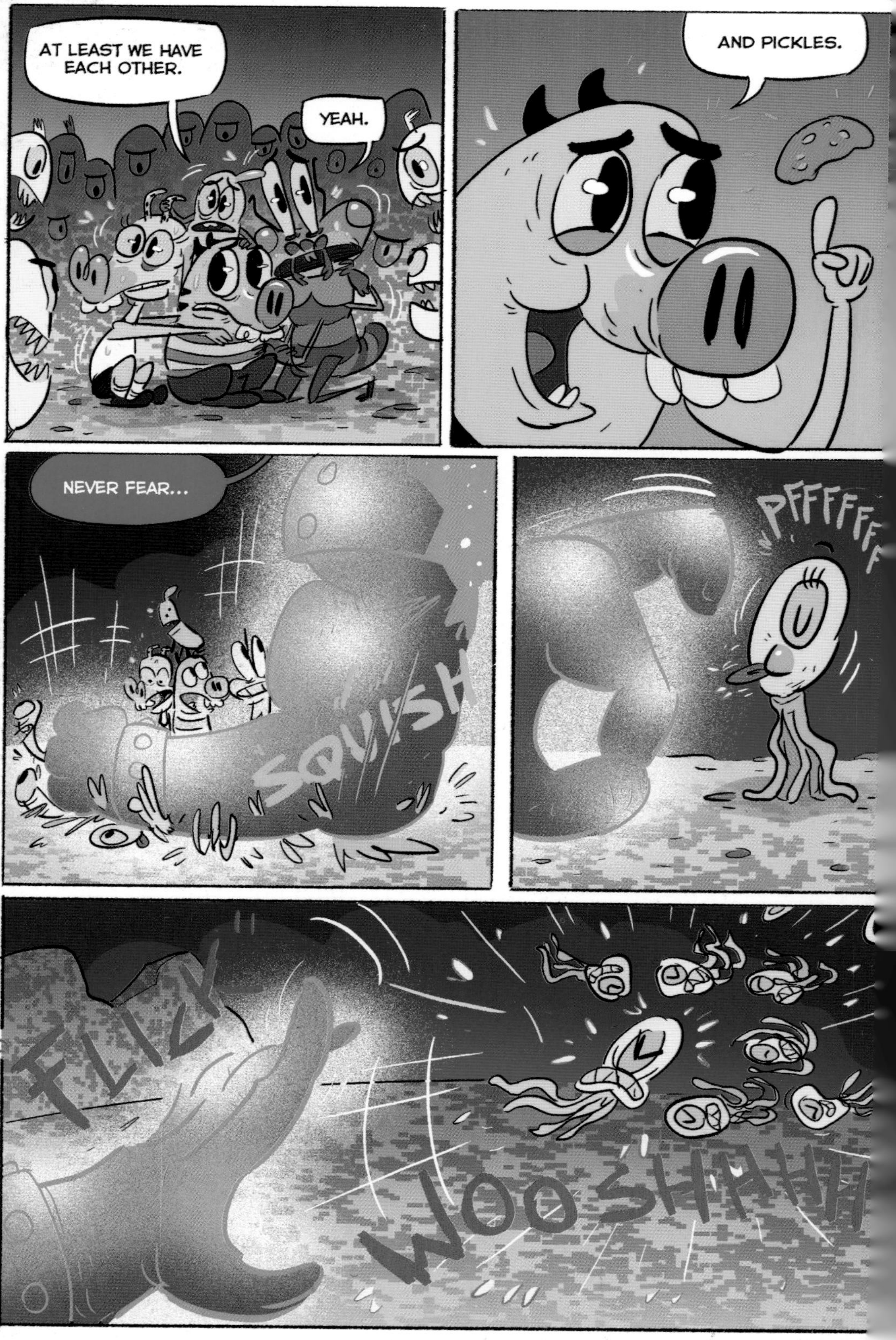
AT LEAST WE HAVE EACH OTHER.
YEAH.
AND PICKLES.
NEVER FEAR...
SQUISH
PFFFFFF
FLICK
WOOSHHHH

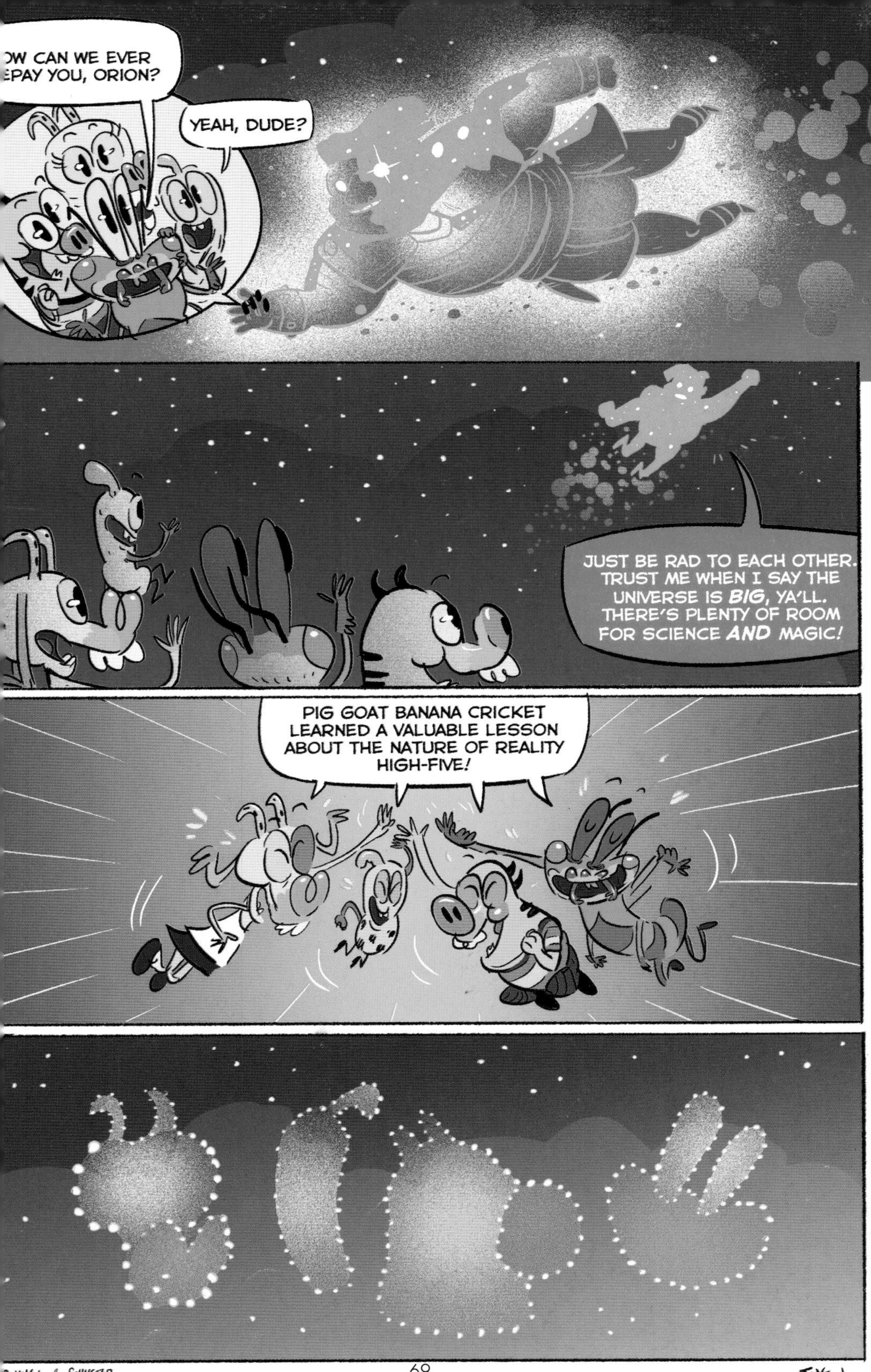
OW CAN WE EVER EPAY YOU, ORION?
YEAH, DUDE?
JUST BE RAD TO EACH OTHER. TRUST ME WHEN I SAY THE UNIVERSE IS BIG, YA'LL. THERE'S PLENTY OF ROOM FOR SCIENCE AND MAGIC!
PIG GOAT BANANA CRICKET LEARNED A VALUABLE LESSON ABOUT THE NATURE OF REALITY HIGH-FIVE!

THE END!

WATCH OUT FOR PAPERCUTZ

Welcome to the tele-communicative, third NICKELODEON PANDEMONIUM! graphic novel from Papercutz, those smart-phc users dedicated to publishing great graphic novels for all ages (and area codes). I'm Jim Salicrup, the Editor-in-Chief and no robot caller, here to offer up a quick overview of the great Nickelodeon graphic novels available now from Papercutz...

For SANJAY AND CRAIG, press one... If you enjoy the SANJAY AND CRAIG show on Nickelodeon and/or the SANJAY AND CRAIG stories in this graphic novel, you'll love the SANJAY AND CRAIG graphic novels—all three of them! Each one packed with 50 pages of new comics featuring all your favorite SANJAY AND CRAIG characters, including Sanjay's parent Vijay and Darlene Patel; friends, Hector Flanagan, Megan Sparkles, Belle and Penny Pepper; plus crazy neighbor Mr. Leslie Noodman; and Sanjay's idol, Remington Tufflips.

For BREADWINNERS, press two... Who can possibly get enough of those two quazy bread-delivering ducks, SwaySway and Buhdeuce? Fortunately, beyond the TV series and the stories in this graphic novel, there are two whole Papercutz graph novels filled with plenty of all-new BREADWINNERS stories! Featuring such Pondgean pals as Jelly, the Bread Maker, Ketta, T-Midi, Rambamboo, plus: Oonski the Great and all sorts of Monsters! SwaySway and Buhdeuce's zeal to deliver bread als translates into their desire to entertain you—they always deliver, and never give up! This series will quack you up!

For HARVEY BEAKS, press three... HARVEY BEAKS is the story of the unlikely friendship between a kid who's never broken rules and his two friends who've never lived by any. If you've enjoyed the TV series and the stories in this graphic novel, and you're looking for more new HARVEY BEAKS stories, you have to get his two graphic novels! You'll love Harvey's adventures with Fee and Foo, as well as Dade, Technobear, Princess, Jeremy, Randl, and many more!

For PIG GOAT BANANA CRICKET, press four... What do a Pig, a Goat, a Banana, and a Cricket have in common? Nothir But that doesn't stop these four best friends from having the time of their lives in a weird and wild city where absolutely anyth goes! They live together, argue with each other, stand up for each other, and even though their adventures may take them on different paths, they always start and end each day as a team! If you love the TV series and/or the comics in this graphic no you'll love the PIG GOAT BANANA CRICKET graphic novel from Papercutz!

For THE LOUD HOUSE, press five... Ever wonder what it's like having a big family? Well, in Nickelodeon's newest animatec series, THE LOUD HOUSE, 11-year-old Lincoln Loud gives you an inside look at what it takes to survive in the chaos of a hug household, especially as the only boy with 10 sisters (Lori, Leni, Luna, Luan, Lynn, Lucy, Lana, Lola, Lisa, and Lily)! The trick to surviving is to remain calm, cool, and collected. But most importantly for Lincoln, you've got to have a plan. With all the chac and craziness, one thing is always for sure: there is never a dull moment in the Loud house! If you love the TV series and/or the comics in this graphic novel (including the preview on the pages following), you'll love THE LOUD HOUSE, the all-new graphic novel series from Papercutz!

For any other Papercutz inquiries, please go to Papercutz.com for more information.

You may hang up now, or just turn the page.

Thank you, Jim

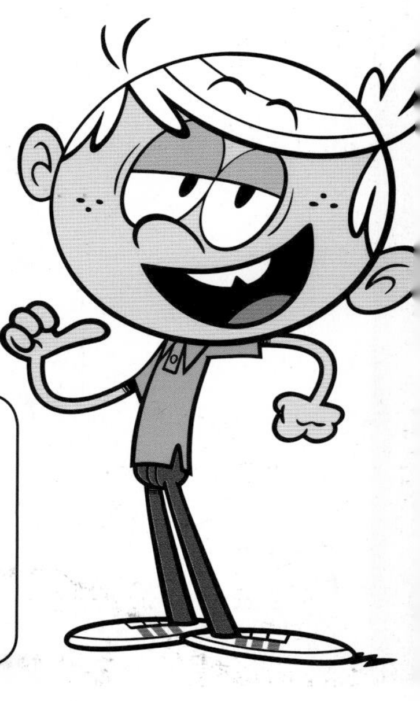

STAY IN TOUCH!

EMAIL:	salicrup@papercutz.com
WEB:	papercutz.com
INSTAGRAM:	@papercutzgn
TWITTER:	@papercutzgn
FACEBOOK:	PAPERCUTZGRAPHICNOVELS
FANMAIL:	Papercutz, 160 Broadway, Suite 700, East Wing, New York, NY 10038

"SHOCKER"

WAWA BABA POO POO KA KA! WHAAAAAAAH!

YOU WERE WATCHING OUR FAVORITE CARTOON SHOW WHEN OUR SIBLINGS TOOK OVER THE T.V. AND LUAN MADE A BAD JOKE?

BAH BAH POO-POO GOO-GOO GA GA.

*TRANSLATION:
"I GOT THIS."

CLOP CLOP

SHUFFLE SHUFFLE SHUFFLE

SHUFFLE SHUFFLE SHUFFLE

SHUFFLE SHUFFLE SHUFFLE

SHUFFLE SHUFFLE SHUFFLE

SHUF SHU SHUF

SHUFFLE SHUFFLE

OLD CARPET

SHUFF SHUFF SHUFF

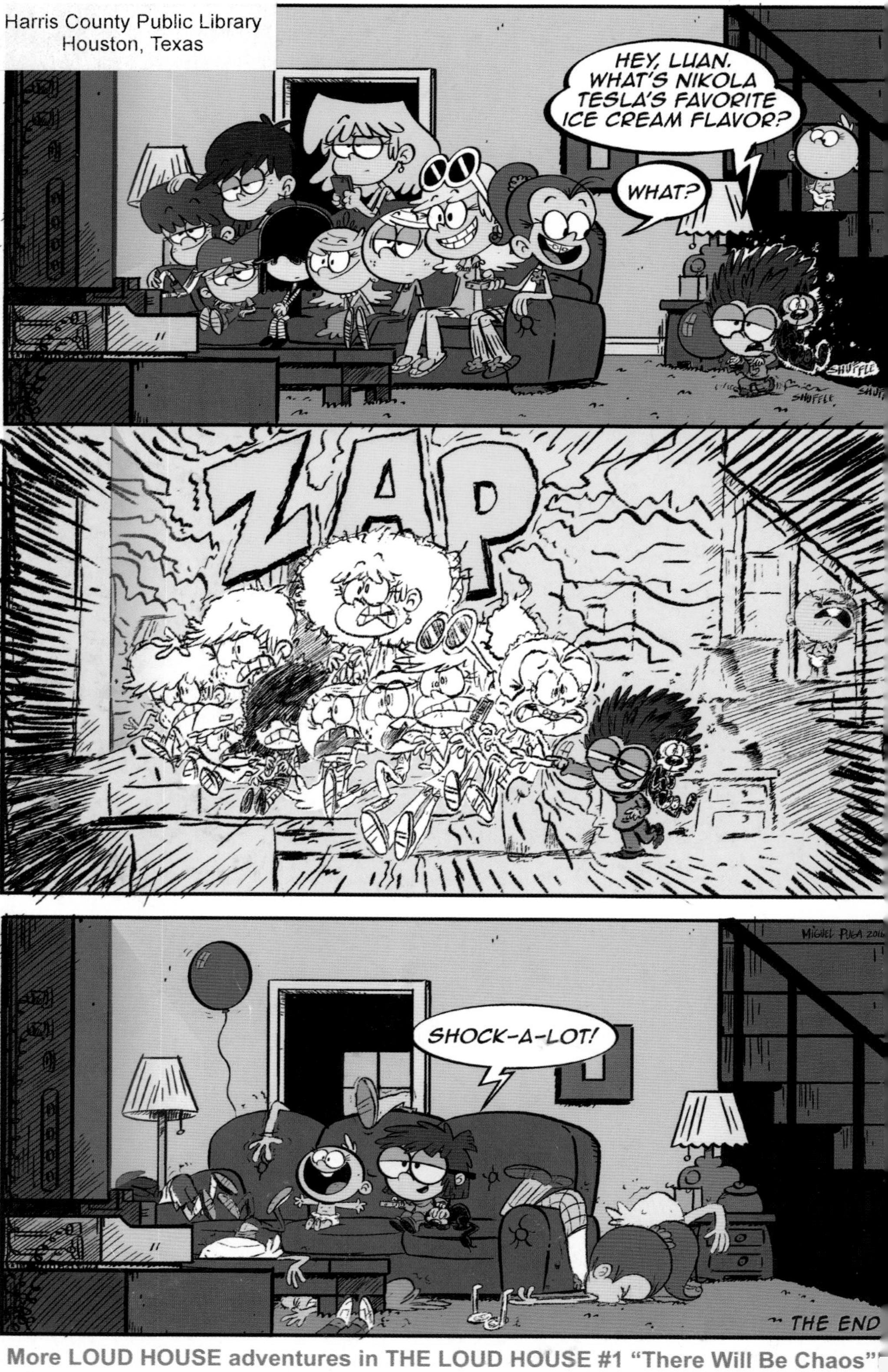
HEY, LUAN. WHAT'S NIKOLA TESLA'S FAVORITE ICE CREAM FLAVOR?
WHAT?
SHUFFLE
SHUFFLE
ZAP
MIGUEL PUGA 2016
SHOCK-A-LOT!
THE END

More LOUD HOUSE adventures in THE LOUD HOUSE #1 "There Will Be Chaos"!